Haunting Blend

A PARAMOUR BAY MYSTERY
BOOK FOUR

KENNEDY LAYNE

KENNEDY LAYNE PUBLISHING, INC.

Dedication

Jeffrey — To my personal protector against all things supernatural...and especially in those haunted houses we enjoy every Halloween!

Cole — To my scary movie partner...I probably started you out younger than I should have!

About the Book

Ghostly antics and magical chaos turn into a hauntingly mischievous tale in this delightful continuation of USA Today Bestselling Author Kennedy Layne's cozy paranormal mystery series...

The small coastal Connecticut town of Paramour Bay has brought a lot of surprises to Raven Marigold's life, but she never expected to encounter a bona fide honest-to-gosh ghost!

It appears that Raven and her familiar have made quite the name for themselves on the other side as amateur sleuths... enticing an endearing tea-drinking spirit to seek their help to solve a kidnapping, of sorts. You see, the sweet apparition's familiar didn't follow her into the afterlife and has gone missing—even from the eyes of the dead!

Grab a cup of hot tea and a cozy blanket so that you can snuggle in front of the warm hearth of your fireplace with this riveting supernatural tale that will have you smiling well into the night!

One

"This time of year always gets to me."

The street lamps that lined River Bay, the main thorough-fare through town, began to light up one by one as dusk encroached earlier each evening. Yes, it was that time of year, and I was a bit melancholy over the fact that the holidays had passed by so fast.

The old-fashioned gas lamp-styled posts gave off a Norman Rockwell vibe, while the antique-tailored awnings of each storefront added to the charming ambiance. Even the cobble-stone intersections gave the impression of being transported back in time to when horse-drawn carriages were commonplace.

I'd come to love the small coastal town of Paramour Bay, Connecticut—population three hundred and fifty-five.

Unfortunately, the days of the local fisherman wringing out a living from the Long Island Sound had passed this town by many years ago. The harsh winter weather we were currently experiencing had the effect of limiting the average enthusiast's taste for a casual cruise in the choppy, cold black waves. The day-trippers had thinned out quite a bit, as well.

The colorful holiday decorations had been collected from their perches on each street post, the townsfolk seemed to have collectively holed up inside their homes after the New Year, and I hadn't had a cup of coffee since early this morning when I left the house.

Don't forget the other reason you're miserable—the good ol' sheriff is out of town for the week.

I didn't react to Leo's wisecrack about Sheriff Liam Drake, because anything I said would only urge my familiar to continue his incessant dialogue as to why my dating anyone at this juncture in my life wasn't the wisest choice for a budding witch.

The thing of it was...it probably *wasn't* the best decision I could have made, but I didn't regret celebrating New Year's Eve with Liam in the least. The celestial tradition of ringing in the new year with an intimate brush of our lips had been worth the price of admission. I also couldn't stop the flush that filled my cheeks nor the smile that blossomed across my face simply thinking about the kiss we'd shared at midnight.

Don't make me nauseous recalling such violations out loud.

"Liam will be back by Friday, when we plan to have a romantic, private dinner at his house," I reminded Leo, flipping the sign to indicate that the tea shop was closed for the evening. "It will be our second date. I want you to stay home and far away this time. I'm serious, Leo. No interruptions. That is an order."

I don't want to jinx you or me, but I was already planning on staying home Friday night sampling some premium organic catnip with my new Savinelli pipe while enjoying the comfort of my new smoking jacket. That is, as long as another dead body doesn't pop up.

"Don't scare the reader away," I scolded Leo, not wanting any of you to get the wrong idea. "These cozy mysteries are worthwhile adventures for our fans."

I should probably take this opportunity to introduce myself before Leo frightens you all away.

I'm pretty sure the mere mention of deceased bodies being discovered did the trick...unless our fan base is into that kind of thing.

Please ignore him. He just got up from a two-hour nap in a discarded cardboard box that I'd left out in the back room.

My name is Raven Lattice Marigold, and I'm a descendant of a long line of witches. In case you've already read the other books in our series, bear with me while I catch the new readers up on the Marigold family history.

Where's my Savinelli? I guess I'll break it in early. I don't need to hear this rubbish again.

Long story short, I didn't always know of my extraordinary heritage. You see, my grandmother and mother had a falling out over our future roles in the supernatural realm. My mother made the terrible decision to keep my family's legacy hidden from me, but secrets always have a way of revealing themselves. And it's also just a nice way of saying one is covering up a lie. Nothing good comes from that. Sooner or later, the truth gets out.

Not if you keep your mouth shut. See how that works?

I can't say that Leo didn't have a point, but it wasn't like someone could conceal the generations upon generations of witches in my family—least of all my mother. It wasn't like we were the only ones around, either. There was an entire coven out there somewhere.

Anyway, can you believe I didn't even know about our family's legacy until Nan died of a heart attack on her daily walk this past October? Her untimely death had been a few weeks before my thirtieth birthday, leaving me with her house, a tea shop, and one heck of a discovery in this small Connecticut town.

Don't forget me this time around. And please tell them to refer to me as Mr. Leo or Sir Leo. Either would be acceptable. A little respect would be a nice change of pace, given your predilection for familiarity.

That's right. Nan also left behind her somewhat peculiar yet well-meaning familiar to help train me. That wasn't the normal process, in case you were wondering, but circumstances being what they were...I ended up with Leo.

A familiar usually crosses to the other side with their host, but Nan used a form of dark magic called necromancy to prevent Leo from joining her in the afterlife. You see, she didn't want me to be alone once I'd found out that I was a witch and that my mother had intentionally hidden it from me.

And in the process of nixing any chance of me enjoying my happily ever after, Rosemary didn't give one iota of thought as to how I would feel being left behind with an accident-prone, half-baked hedge witch or leaving me looking like young Master Frankenstein's first attempt at pet reanimation. With that said, I'm used to modeling this fantastic bod now—GQ material all the way, including the grunge look.

You can imagine my surprise when my departed grandmother's odd cat began to speak to me in words that only I could hear in my head. I literally thought I was losing my mind. You see, I can hear Leo in my head, though all everyone else hears is his meowing...beside other witches, that is. It makes it rather hard to appear sane in front of normal people when I'm hearing a conversation that includes Leo's witty commentary.

As for Leo's appearance...well.

Go ahead. Tell them. If dead bodies haven't scared them away, neither will the fact that my whiskers are slightly crooked, my tail is rather bent, my beautiful orange and black fur has a few tufts that my tongue can't manage to smooth out, and my left eye is a tad larger than my right—it shows character.

Yep. That sums it up.

"You make it sound as if dead bodies are popping up all over the place. I'll have you know that only two murders have occurred since I moved here, and one of the deceased didn't have anything to do with me or my lack of witchcraft mastery."

You've lived in Paramour Bay for three months. Two bodies in three months. You don't have to be good at math to figure out those odds aren't exactly mutually exclusive.

"Don't I get credit for solving those cases?" I asked, closing out the cash register for Monday's meager earnings. As I'd mentioned before, foot traffic had been rather slow since Christmas. Thank goodness for Nan's little black market side business in homeopathic blends of tea. The willing imbibers paid a premium price for those ingredients. "You have to admit, I'm getting a little bit better at casting enchanting spells and recreating Nan's magical blends."

You technically didn't solve either one of those murders. The answers fell into your lap. The cases just sort of unraveled while you were standing in the way, if you want the honest truth.

"You're just grouchy that Heidi didn't visit us this past weekend."

Heidi Connolly was my best friend, currently residing in New York City where I used to live. She usually came to visit twice a month, but her job as an accountant was bound to keep her away for most of the next three months with tax season in full swing.

Oh, you know that rule about witches not sharing their secret with anyone outside the covens? Well, I kind of broke it... by accident.

Kind of an accident? You realize that this isn't a game of checkers, right?

Okay, so I told Heidi that I was a witch, because she's my BFF. Nothing bad happened. The house didn't catch fire, Leo didn't spontaneously combust, and the catnip didn't explode.

Whoa there, Nellie. You're just blazing a new trail in witchcraft, is that it?

"So what if I am blazing a new trail? It's not like anyone handed me a manual on my first day," I deflected, walking across the tea shop to the back room where I kept my winter dress coat. I parted the delicate strings of carved ivory-colored fairies that kept the customers from peering into the storage room and entered the back area. The beads were in fact enchanted to keep onlookers from hearing or seeing into my behind-the-scenes sanctuary—with the exception of Leo, of course. "Even you have to admit it makes it easier on us to have Heidi in the loop."

It would be even better if you told her about Beetle's rather interesting development.

"I don't want to stress Heidi out by telling her our local accountant here in Paramour Bay is getting ready to retire. Heidi's got a heart of gold and would never leave her firm shorthanded before tax season ends." I grabbed my jacket and then made sure the door that led out to the delivery area out back was bolted. "Besides, I heard that Beetle is going to keep his accounting firm open until the end of April. I promise that I'll talk to Heidi right beforehand. She's always dreamed of owning her own small business, so maybe she'll want to take it over. I want her close by, too, Leo."

I expected Leo to say something philosophical about me waiting too long to bring up the subject, but he remained quiet. Who knows? Maybe he'd found his pipe, after all. Either way, he could appear and disappear at will. He was usually one step ahead of me and already lying on his pillow in the front window by the time I parked my beat-up old Corolla in front of the house Nan had left me on the not-so-far edge of town.

I should also mention that Leo fancies Heidi quite a bit and that he isn't happy that she started dating a detective with the state police by the name of Jack Swanson. Leo would claim that Jack wasn't right for her, but I disagree. His dependable nature and charismatic smile are good for her. She's been doing a lot more smiling lately, too.

"Leo? Are you still waiting for me?" I slipped back through the ivory-colored fairies, the melodic clicking sound rather comforting. "I was thinking that we could—"

I came up short, not quite sure my vision wasn't playing tricks on me.

A few blinks warned me otherwise, and a lump began to form in the back of my throat. I was kind of blindsided that the palm of my hand hadn't given me a warning that Leo and I might be in danger. I usually had a prognostic sense for threats, but it was clear that something had short-circuited my unusual awareness.

Don't. Say. A. Word.

Not only didn't I verbally say anything, I also didn't move a muscle. I was afraid any slightest movement would cause the apparition in front of me to do something abrupt that I wasn't ready to deal with. Using only my eyes, I could see Leo sitting still as a statue next to the cash register. His left eye was not only larger than his right, it was now literally bulging out of its socket.

It was never a good thing when Leo was this wary of a mystical situation. Unless, of course, it had to do with the appearance of dead bodies. The vision in front of me was pretty darn close to that, as far as those kinds of things went.

I was almost afraid to breathe, but it was either drag some oxygen into my lungs or pass out cold.

Pass out. I vote for avoiding this whole mess.

I didn't like that option, so I chose to slowly inhale as I refocused my sights on...

Go ahead. Say it. Blurt it out. You might as well let the cat out of the bag.

An honest to goodness...ghost!

Two

I was literally staring at a poltergeist—you know, a semitransparent floating apparition. I would have questioned my sanity, but I'd already proven to myself that I wasn't slowly going mad on more than one occasion. Nonetheless, it did make me wonder how I continually got myself into these extraordinary predicaments, especially when my life had once been so mundane.

I obviously couldn't continue to stand frozen right outside the storage room without moving. I'd definitely appear odd, considering that anyone outside the shop could clearly see inside with all the overhead lights on. I briefly wondered if the passersby could see the somewhat opaque woman sitting at one of the high-top tables or did only Leo and I have that unique pleasure?

Oh, boy. This wasn't good.

You should continue to stand there and not attract its attention. That's the smart thing to do. The pesky old hag will disappear soon enough, and then we can get ourselves out of here.

Ghosts can only sustain so much energy to remain visible. You should know that by now!

No, I didn't know that, because Leo had neglected to inform me that ghosts could—

Did you not read over those assignments Rosemary left for you? With my condition, I can't be expected to remember everything, you know. And don't you dare throw me under the bus. I'm pretty sure we had a discussion about the inn being haunted, but you didn't want to hear anything about it at the time. So, let me make this perfectly clear—If you don't move and alert the ghost to your presence, we might stand a chance of avoiding a crash course in spiritual divination.

Now Leo manages to remember what he said so many weeks ago? And just so you know, he never gave me a message about a reading assignment from Nan.

I didn't?

Shoot. I totally forgot to share with you that the black magic Nan had used—a necromancy spell, to be exact—to prevent Leo from crossing over to the other side hadn't only affected his physical appearance...it had also caused short-term memory loss.

Unfortunately, it was an unintended side effect that served as a consequence for exploiting magic deemed too dark to be used by mere mortals. Those nightmares and folktales from the old days aren't just make believe, after all.

I'm going to correct myself here, seeing as I didn't want to deal with what was in front of me just quite yet. Leo's memory loss tended to affect his memory in general and at the most inopportune times.

What caused a spine-tingling cautious warning that it was too late to run was the frown on the older woman's weathered features. It was almost as if she were reacting to every word that Leo and I said, but that couldn't be right.

The ghostly figure was not only currently sitting at one of my high-top tables, she was also presumably enjoying a cup of steaming hot tea.

Well, sort of.

She was there, but then again...she wasn't entirely.

Oh, she's there, alright. You're about to find out exactly how much there *she is.*

It was as if the woman was made of mist, yet I could clearly see the vivid colors of her stylish floppy hat and floral dress. I had to admit that the pink shade suited her. She reminded me of one of those English royal women who dressed up to drink their afternoon tea, pinky up and everything just like those etiquette schools used to teach back in the day.

Wait.

Ghosts could drink?

I could certainly use a drink myself right about now. Bourbon, maybe.

Leo wasn't helping the situation, and I couldn't stand here for the rest of the night. I'd been in the process of putting on my dress coat when I'd walked through the strings of ivory-colored fairies, and my body was at an odd angle. I gradually lowered my arms and purposefully gripped my coat in my left hand.

There were times I could gather enough energy in my left palm to use while protecting myself, but I wasn't so sure it would help either of us in this case.

I hate to break it to you, but there's not a thing you can do if that ghost decides to stir up any funny business.

Funny business? Recollections of various horror films involving demons and ghosts certainly weren't helping me contain my fear. Did I even want to know what a spirit or poltergeist could do when unhappy?

Trust me, that is a definitive non-starter.

"Are the two of you going to keep conversing with one another or can this old witch spirit get a word in edgewise?"

I admit, I did scream.

Sort of.

It was a small squeal that sounded like I'd stepped on Leo's tail. I'm not proud that it escaped my lips, but it happened all the same.

Leo instinctively vanished so fast that tufts of his orange and black hair were still floating in the air where he'd been.

"Maybe I'm in the wrong place, but Rosemary assured me that *Tea, Leaves, & Eves* was the tea shop where her grand-daughter worked," the older lady shared before setting her cup of tea down on the delicate saucer. She met my gaze, causing another wave of panic to wash over me. "Are you the infamous Raven Lattice Marigold?"

I opened my mouth to answer, but nothing came out. It was a silly thing to focus on, but I made the realization that the china she was using also held a misty sort of quality. Go figure. That particular tea set must have come from the other side, as well. It would have been a top seller here in the shop.

That wasn't the only thing that caught my attention, and I was finally able to say something other than standing there looking like a fish out of water.

"You know my Nan?"

A million thoughts ran through my mind at once, but I wasn't sure where to begin. If this woman was from the other side, then why couldn't my Nan pay me a visit? What was a ghost doing in my tea shop in the first place? Could I somehow talk to—

"Oh, don't get your knickers in a bunch, dearie. I'll answer all your questions in due time." The feminine apparition raised an eyebrow in question as she looked around the shop. "Where did your funny-looking familiar go? There are some things we need to discuss, and I don't have all day."

I wasn't sure what there was to discuss with a ghost, but I also realized that it was probably a bad idea to upset her, given my current position.

There was only one thing to do.

"Leo." I waited for him to appear, but he remained invisible. "Leo, show yourself right this minute."

I was not going to be left alone with an apparition of which I understood nothing about.

Technically, there wasn't much I could do if Leo decided to remain unseen, but I'd continue to badger him until he did the right thing. After all, Nan had left him behind to help me, and I was clearly out of my element at the moment.

You remember my fear of spiders? Well, ghosts rank right up there with those eight-legged creatures.

"Are you comparing me to a hairy, long-legged spider, Mr. Leo?"

Leo suddenly reappeared, and his chest slightly rose as he took in the title that he pretty much demanded everyone call him.

I love her.

Great.

She just had to coddle his mammoth ego.

It wasn't a surprise when Leo leapt off the counter and began sauntering toward the misty poltergeist in long strides that had his bent tail swaying back and forth in the most graceful manner he could muster.

What is your name, my darling witch?

I rolled my eyes and shook my head at Leo's change of heart at talking and interacting with such a fearsome spirit. Of course, he would change his tune now that she'd given him exactly what he'd wanted—reverence.

Don't ruin my moment, Raven.

"Rosemary said that you were quite the charmer, Mr. Leo," the elderly specter said with a light laugh. Her oversized hat flapped a bit as she rested her fingers against her neck in delight. "My name is Mazie Rose Young, and I've come to hire the two of you to solve a mystical mystery."

I remember you now. You're one of Rosemary's friends from her time at the coven. How have you been, Mazie?

Now that Leo had moved closer to the table, I slowly followed behind. He'd greeted her like an old friend, but it was easy to see that the word *mystery* had put a little hitch in Leo's step. He continued to move toward the table, anyway.

I couldn't help but cast a quick glance toward the window, afraid I'd find someone peering in and wondering why it looked as if I was speaking to a vacant chair.

Okay. I might have also been looking for a reflection. Silly me...ghosts don't have reflections.

I decided it was best to find out what this ghost wanted and send her on her merry way. I'd wait to deal with the fact that ghosts could interact with living humans after a few glasses of wine.

"Pardon me, but did you say that you've come to hire us for..." I had to have heard the apparition wrong, even though Ms. Young had spoken rather clearly. There were times that the haze of mist became more solid, which told me that her spirit was struggling with some unknown force to remain in our realm of existence. "I'm sorry. I thought you said you wanted us to solve a mystery of some sort."

Don't do it.

I snatched my hand back, tucking both arms underneath my coat.

Touching an apparition might just cause you a severe case of frostbite.

Leo's warning had me shooting him an annoyed glance. How had he known I was about to reach out to see if I could touch Mazie's arm? I mean, wouldn't you be curious, too?

No. Most ordinary people run from ghosts.

"That's right, dear. There's a mystery I need you to solve." Mazie patted the other stool, but she'd done so in order to let Leo know he was more than welcome to join her at the table. He didn't hesitate and somehow was able to leap the four feet onto the cushion with ease. He wasn't what one would consider a lightweight kitty. "Now, let's get back to business. You understand how hard it is for me to stay here for long periods of time, Mr. Leo."

How is Rosemary?

I flicked my gaze back and forth between them in astonishment. Were they really going to carry on a conversation as if this was a normal visit by an old friend from beyond the grave?

"Oh, that woman has been stirring up trouble during her transition. Last I heard, Rosemary was complaining about the bread, though I have no idea why. It's quite good, you know. The manna over there fulfills one's every need. It reminds me of a fresh croissant, warm out of the oven." Mazie reached for her tea as she and Leo continued to casually converse as if talking with the dead was an everyday activity. Hadn't she just said that she didn't have time for small talk? "Now don't go worrying about Rosemary. That woman can take care of herself, and she's fitting right in. I'm certain she'll find a reason to visit once she's completed her transition."

It figures. I could be there with her in all my glory as a Persian leopard, yet she left me behind as if I was nothing but a mere housecat with...issues.

I'll admit that my shock at seeing an actual bona fide spirit might have hampered my ability to fully understand what was happening right in front of me, but it was time for me to grow a backbone. This discussion was getting away from the subject Mazie had paid us a visit for in the first place.

"Um, Ms. Young," I began, attempting to hide my hesitation. How did one go about conversing with a ghost like they were actually there in person? Leo didn't seem to have a problem, but I found it rather disconcerting. I cleared my throat to make sure she understood me. "Why have you come to us in particular? Why seek us out of all the living?"

Stop that. You sound as if we're attempting to conduct a séance. It's rude.

"We can do that?" I asked in surprise, not meaning to veer from the topic of conversation once again, but this was too good to pass up. "As in, use a Ouija board to talk with Nan?"

"Now those things are quite tricky, Raven," Mazie warned with a wag of her finger. "That's a portal that you should be very wary of in your craft. You never truly know whom you're talking to on the other side. If in fact, it's a human spirit at all."

I couldn't have said it better myself. Thank you, Mazie.

I inhaled deeply, attempting to control my irritation that these two were getting along like two peas in a pod after Leo practically demanded I ignore the haunting poltergeist to begin with.

And it didn't escape me that Leo had mentioned he'd known her when she was...well, not a ghost. He'd never mentioned Ms. Young before, and neither had anyone else in

16

town. So, who was she and why hadn't I ever heard about her before?

"Ms. Young, why are you—"

"Oh, please call me Mazie, dearie. The only one who used to call me Ms. Young were those witches and wizards on the council," Mazie shared with a dismissive shake of head. It was clear she didn't approve of the council, but it made me all the more curious to find out if she was talking about the so-called coven I had yet to meet another member of. "I swear, those old relics are to blame for me going to such an early grave."

Leo and I both gasped, believing that Mazie meant the coven's council was to blame for her death. Was that the reason she was here? Was she looking for justice? Was she calling on all the witches in this area to help her find the culprit? Oh, wow. This was way out of my league.

Tell me about it. No one goes up against the so-called "Wise Ones" and walks away clean.

"Mr. Leo, it's been quite a while since we've seen each other. I would tell you about how difficult the council made my life after Rosemary and I lost touch in the human realm, but we just don't have time. There's been a lot of turnover on the council, in case you weren't aware." Mazie paused long enough to have another sip of tea, though I wasn't quite certain that she was consuming an actual beverage. Maybe she was just going through the motions? The cup made a tangible sound as it clanked against the saucer. "Let's get down to business, shall we?"

"And what business is that, Mazie?"

I found it very hard to call someone by their first name who was so elderly and...

Dead?

I shot Leo another exasperated look.

I'm just keeping it real.

"You two are all everyone on the other side is talking about during social events," Mazie gushed, waving her hand as if she couldn't believe she was in the same room with us.

Truthfully, I couldn't believe we were in this situation, either, but for many different reasons.

Hush now, girl. I like being treated like royalty. Mazie, do go on.

"I'm just saying that the stories of how you two amateur sleuths keep solving crimes using witchcraft have taken over high tea. Who would have guessed that the two of you would be so good at cracking mysteries?" Mazie leaned forward and lowered her voice to a whisper as if we were conspiring against the world. It seemed only natural for Leo and me to lean in, also. "I'm surprised the council hasn't reached out to you to solve the unexplained thefts that have taken place in the worship temple as of late, but I digress. I'm here because of Strifle."

Strifle?

"Strifle?"

It wasn't uncommon for Leo and me to echo each other's words, but it was usually because one of us didn't understand what the other was talking about. In this case? We were both lost for a meaning.

And here I thought Leo was a strange name for a cat.

I just remembered something important. This isn't good. Oh, this isn't good at all!

It appeared that Leo wasn't so lost in this turn of events as I was now that his memory had been jogged.

"Yes, Strifle," Mazie answered with an affirmative nod. She took a moment to use a handkerchief that had come out of nowhere to dab the corners of her eyes. It was obvious she was upset about whatever happened to Strifle, but it was rather hard to keep up with the conversation when I had no idea what it was about. "You see, my familiar didn't cross over with me to the other side."

Listen to me very carefully, Raven. We're going to have to back away slowly while avoiding eye contact.

"Your familiar is named Strifle?" I straightened, not understanding why Leo's orange and black fur was slowly rising one by one as he inched toward the left side of the stool. "Where is Strifle now?"

Have you learned nothing these past three months? Don't ask questions you don't want answers to!

"What are you talking about?" I couldn't help but inquire in response to Leo's dramatized reaction. I even switched my gaze from Mazie to Leo and then back again. It was obvious that they both knew something I didn't. "Leo, do you know Strifle?"

I feel a hairball in the back of my throat.

"But—"

I'll say it again—slowly back away from the table and never speak of this again.

"Mr. Leo, don't you think you're overreacting?" Mazie said in disappointment, her frown causing me concern. Unhappy ghosts were one of the reasons sidekick characters usually died in horror flicks. What did Leo think he was doing, stirring up trouble like this? "Strifle isn't like the others."

"Others?" I cautiously asked, completely terrified that Leo and I had found ourselves up a creek without a paddle once more.

You're just now figuring that one out?

This wasn't something I could ignore, now was it? After

all, it was the reason Mazie felt the need to cross that veil between our worlds.

I could admit to loving the adrenaline that came with solving a mystery, but I could definitely do without the close calls with death that both Leo and I had experienced. Talking to a ghost ranked right up there in the *bad idea* column, and clearly Strifle wasn't simply a cat.

Don't. Do. It.

"What exactly is Strifle?"

You just had to ask, didn't you? You couldn't listen to me just this once, could you? Now we're doomed. Doomed, I tell you. Oh, boy. I need a puff or two of my best catnip. Where's my pipe?

Three

"Strifle is a fairy, of course," Mazie replied as if it were the most common type of familiar in the supernatural world—next to cats, of course. She even widened her eyes as if we'd surprised her with our question. "It's all in her name—strife. See what I did there? Strifle is such a cute name for a pixie, and I do miss her so. You can imagine my surprise when I crossed over last month and she wasn't with me. Did you know that fairies are known for—"

Discord? Causing dissention wherever they go? Yes, I'm familiar with fairies, and they're nothing but trouble.

"Are we talking about something like a Tinkerbell kind of fairy?" I found a pixie with little gossamer wings rather endearing. "They're so cute!"

Cute? Cute?!? Raven, I'm having issues breathing again. It's definitely not a hairball this time. I need medicinal grade catnip, STAT!

I wasn't going to ask what was causing Leo's breathing problem, because it was a well-known fact that he had panic attacks anytime anything this exciting happened. I was more concerned with what Mazie wanted us to do about a missing fairy. Finding her would be the obvious answer, but I had no clue where to start looking for a missing familiar.

Nothing. We do nothing, do you hear me? Fairies are bad news from the word go.

"Mr. Leo, may I remind you that Strifle isn't like other fairies?" Mazie arched her right eyebrow high enough to reach the brim of her hat. "She might have a bit of a mischievous side, but she's not malicious. Nor would she abandon me of her own free will. I think the council members had something to do with Strifle's abduction."

Back up the horse! You call purposefully giving me wrong directions in the woods mischievous? I could have died out there! I'm not equipped for living in the forest!

Obviously, Leo and Strifle had somehow been acquainted in the past. He'd have to share his stories at home, because pixies aside—along with Leo's opinion of their ilk—it probably wasn't wise for us to get involved with a...kidnapping? I mean, what else could it be? Leo and I weren't the mystic police, regardless of what the other side was referring to as our passable sleuthing skills. Giving a helping hand to Liam or Detective Swanson was completely different than taking on the lead role in an investigation.

Now that's calling the kettle black. No pun intended, but it was you who led the witch hunt to clear Rosemary's name of being involved in a fifty-three-year-old murder. How did that turn out for you?

"That was different," I whispered to Leo in admonishment, not wanting to discuss past events in front of a ghost who might very well go to the other side and tell Nan about everything I'd done. "You aren't being much of a help right now."

I'm the one telling you we need to send Mazie on her way. Thanks, but no thanks. That's me...helping. The old bat has nothing under that flimsy hat if she believes fairies aren't chaos incarnate. Ohhhhhh. I just remembered something else.

"Of course, you did," I said wryly, bracing myself for what Leo was about to say. I was also trying to remember that Mazie could hear every word that Leo said to me, which was really rather hard now that I'd gotten into the habit of being the only one to converse with him. "What did you remember?"

Witches who keep fairies as familiars are known to be...well, they also play tricks.

"What in heaven's name are you talking about, Mr. Leo?" Mazie asked, fanning herself as if she'd just been given a compliment.

Well, didn't Leo's realization put us in quite a dilemma?

If he was right, how was I to know that anything Mazie said had anything to do with the truth? Then again, would a spirit go to all this trouble to spend enough energy to cross the veil in order to mess with another witch?

May I remind you that we're talking about a witch and her fairy? Fairies are derived from chaos. They are the physical embodiment of the winds of change. They shouldn't have used a butterfly to describe the effect of a pixie beatings its wings and the storm that results on the other side of the world. I'm telling you... they're worse than djinn!

"Mazie, can you...um...how do I put this?" I scratched my head as I tried to come up with a polite way to ask if the older spirit could move. As in, literally move her body so that we weren't in full view of anyone strolling past. It would be better for us to talk in private, where no one could walk in on us. "Are you able to—"

Both Leo and I startled for the second time this evening as

the bell over the door chimed, alerting us that we had a visitor. How was I going to get us out of this mess?

This is it. I'm finally dying. My heart just stopped. Raven, it's been a pleasure to serve with you.

"Raven, is Leo okay?" Eileen Weepler asked as she came flying through the glass door. I mean, not literally. Eileen wasn't a witch or a poltergeist. She was an everyday citizen of Paramour Bay. After reading about me and Leo having a conversation with a ghost and discovering there are actual fairies in the world, I didn't want you to think Eileen could actually fly through glass. "I was walking to my car when I saw you consoling Leo. Is something wrong with him? Does he need to go to the vet? I can call Dr. Jameson for him."

I realize that I probably looked a bit stricken with all-out panic, but what was a girl to do when caught red-handed with a ghost? A quick glance had me practically sagging with relief to find that Mazie had simply evaporated from her seat, taking her teacup and matching saucer with her.

Act normal, Raven. And just so you know, Dr. Jameson and his ice-cold hands aren't coming anywhere near me. Have you seen the size of those needles in his office?

I really needed to act as if everything was fine...even though it wasn't.

As for Dr. Jameson, I would never subject Leo to a human veterinarian or technically, the veterinarian to Leo. I wasn't sure which would incur injury from such an encounter. With that said, I did have to wonder if Leo shouldn't see some witch's doctor who specialized in familiars and their maladies.

I go once a year for my regular checkup, thank you. Now go for the Emmy, Raven. It's yours for the taking. I need to go home and sleep for the next twelve hours after the day I've had. You're completely exhausting, you know that?

"Leo had a hairball stuck in his throat," I explained with a tight smile, trying not to inhale the heavy perfume Eileen liked to douse herself with in the morning. The stuff never seemed to fade, either. "I was worried he couldn't breathe, but he seems fine now."

Would Eileen buy my cover story?

Does a cat shed? Work it, Raven.

"It was so sweet of you to check in on Leo and me," I gushed, probably overdoing it, but Eileen was beaming with pleasure at my compliment. It was time to switch the subject and remove her focus from Leo. "Wasn't that New Year's Eve party that Alison and Oliver Bend hosted over at the wax museum fantastic? I've never had so much fun!"

Just so you know, I'm probably the worst liar in Paramour Bay. My inability to lie made being a witch rather difficult, but I'd somehow succeeded thus far.

There has definitely been a bump or two in the road. Could we hurry this along? You need to tell Mazie that we're not—I repeat, not—in the fairy business. We will not be sending out a search party for that devilish pixie she's gone and lost. Oh, there it is again—arrhythmia. I do need an urgent puff or two.

The bump in the road Leo had been referring to was when I'd told Heidi about my family's secret, but that didn't count. She was my best friend, and I couldn't keep her in the dark about something so important.

That wasn't a bump. It was a volcano, complete with an avalanche, pyroclastic flow, and burning lava. You just haven't heard the shockwaves yet.

"It's been years since Alison and Oliver hosted such an extravagant event," Eileen gushed, though I'd already been informed of that little tidbit. She hadn't buttoned up her jacket, so it hung open at the seams. At first, I thought maybe she was still wearing one of her Christmas sweaters with the bells sewn strategically into the fabric. Upon closer inspection, the sweater was of three dancing snowmen wearing top hats. "The wax museum's reception hall looked gorgeous with that huge ball and streamers hanging from the ceiling, didn't it? And just so you know, all anyone can talk about is that kiss you and Liam shared at midnight."

I might barf, and it has nothing to do with hairballs.

Eileen pretended to fan herself similar to how Mazie had, but this time with different intent. She even gave me a wink of encouragement, but her comment made me slightly uncomfortable considering Eileen wasn't a regular confidant of mine.

I didn't like being the talk of the town, especially when it came to who I was dating. One thing usually led to another, and before you knew it...all one's secrets were laid bare on the table.

Loose lips sink ships. Zip it. I don't want to go down with the Titanic. I don't swim very well.

Granted, the town's police dispatcher had never given any indication that she suspected me of being anything other than a tea shop owner and the granddaughter of Rosemary Lattice Marigold. Unfortunately, I hadn't been at the top of my game lately.

You think? Talk about underestimating yourself. Keep going. You're on a roll.

"Liam and I had a wonderful time," I began, not sure where to cut off this conversation. A part of me was afraid Mazie would reappear, but in all honesty, my mouth would most likely end up being the culprit that got me and Leo ousted to the community. "Heidi and Jack enjoyed the evening, as well. It was good to see Heidi enjoying herself after her previous boyfriend, Patrick, ran off to Maui with one of the baristas at the coffee place they'd frequent on the weekends. She's better off without someone of his maturity."

Now who is spreading gossip?

"That poor girl," Eileen declared with a shake of her head. "Heidi is such a doll. You know, it's all over town that Beetle is retiring. She should set up shop here with us. I'm sure you know by now that all of the business owners are worried about who they're going to find to do their taxes, payroll, and handle such matters. Do you think that Heidi would be interested in taking over Beetle's clientele?"

Yes, yes, yes! I'm not the only one who wants that blonde goddess nearby.

"Otis told me a couple of weeks ago that Beetle is retiring. I'm waiting for an opportune time to bring up the subject." Truthfully, I hadn't even known who Beetle was until the former sheriff had pointed him out one morning. The man with the white hair drove a Volkswagen and that was apparently how he'd gotten his name, but he wasn't a tea drinker. I'd only ever seen the man from afar, but he did remind me of that mad scientist in the movie *Back to the Future*. "I'll definitely check with Heidi, but I should probably wait until she can give it some serious thought. January through May is always her busiest time of the year, as you can imagine."

Eileen nodded her understanding before frowning.

"It's rather cold in here, Raven. Is there something wrong with your furnace?"

Now that Eileen mentioned it, the temperature in the shop had dropped rather significantly.

Really? You have to think on that one?

So, it *was* true that the air around an individual dropped precipitately upon a visit from a lost spirit.

Oh, trust me. Mazie's not lost. She came here for a very

specific reason, but I'm not so sure she's telling us the whole truth. Why would the council want to kidnap a fairy?

"I'm not sure why it's so cold in here, but I'll take a look at the thermostat before we head home." I decided now was the perfect time to call an end to the evening. It didn't take me long to slip my arms into my dress coat, signaling that it was time for us to leave. "Eileen, thank you so much for checking on us."

Oh, yeah. She had no hesitation in subjecting me to Dr. Jameson. I should put a needle in her—

"You drive safe now," I advised with a smile, cutting off Leo before he continued down a path that would invite bad karma though an open door. We'd already attracted Mazie's attention, and from what Leo said...I sure didn't want to have anything to do with Strife. "The roads are still a little slick from the dusting we received this morning."

"You do the same, dear. And just so you know, Liam is due back at two o'clock on Friday afternoon. I'll let you know if his schedule changes," Eileen informed me with a bright smile as she zipped up her jacket. I realize that Paramour Bay was a small town, but when did one date make two people a couple? Not that I was opposed to that idea. There was something about Liam that caused my heart to flutter every time I heard his name. Now was no different. "Have a good night!"

Leo and I remained where we were as Eileen vacated the tea shop. We both waited in silence for Mazie to reappear, but ever so slowly the temperature began to return to normal.

"Is she gone?" I asked cautiously, not wanting to disturb the ambiance.

You're asking me? Does it look like I have a P.K.E. meter, Dr. Venkman?

I'd kept my tone soft in order to not jinx anything. I'd never encountered a ghost before, and I wasn't sure I wanted Mazie to come back or stay away. I still had a ton of questions, mostly about Nan, but I wouldn't have any of them answered if Mazie didn't return to continue our conversation.

It's better to keep things status quo. We don't want to upset the balance.

Leo sniffed the air, twitching his bent whiskers all over the place. I waited for him to reach his conclusion. I mean, Mazie seemed harmless. Then again, Leo was the one who'd had experience with fairies before, not to mention spirits from the other side.

Trouble with a capital T.

Another minute passed before either one of us moved, and it was Leo whose orange and black fur began to settle and reassure me that we weren't about to have another tea party. Who would have thought I would be partly disappointed that Mazie hadn't stayed around to talk more?

Don't encourage that old witch! It's your fault we've been given the reputation of being amateur sleuths in the first place. Now every half-baked spirit with an issue is going to be knocking down our door.

I turned away to walk back to the counter in order to retrieve my purse and car keys, not wanting Leo to see my smile. Amateur sleuths? It was kind of cute that the news had reached the other side, and my initial reaction to this entire ghost encounter made me realize how far I'd come over the last three months.

You mean that time when you were ready to commit yourself to a mental institution for hearing a talking cat? "Something like that," I said with a laugh, the melancholy from before completely vanishing. I had been given a brand-new lease on life, and each day was a blessing. There was no reason for me to be sad the holidays were over, and it was time for me to finally make my New Year's resolution. Technically, I'd already made one without even realizing it. "Leo, I'm—"

Don't say it.

"But—"

Do you know how many witches pass over to the other side who aren't ready to go? The last thing we need is to have a long line of incensed spirits wanting us to investigate whatever matter it is they believe were left unresolved. Not happening. No. We're not getting involved.

"I read somewhere that burning sage might keep ghosts away," I offered in reassurance, because we clearly got our wires crossed. I might have handled an interaction with a ghost without screaming my head off, but that didn't mean I wanted to be a conduit for the other side. I was with Leo on this one, which was quite rare. "I have some sage at home, and we'll light it first thing after you've found your pipe."

Then what was it you were going to say?

Leo's tail twitched in irritation as his left eye focused solely on me, most likely wondering what the catch was with my peace offering. It was unusual that I was able to leave him speechless, but I had certainly succeeded with my bombshell.

"I'm going to hire an assistant!"

Four

"What exactly do you mean when you say Mazie Rose Young paid you a visit?" my mother asked me warily over my cell phone. Don't get me wrong. I realized my mistake right away, but it was too late to rectify the upcoming lecture. "I'd heard she'd passed away over a month ago. Are you saying you've talked with her since?"

I should never have taken my mother's phone call before I'd made it into the house, but it had been instinctive to answer since I'd just pulled my beat-up old Corolla alongside the wrought iron fence that surrounded the cottage I'd inherited from my Nan.

My second major error in judgement had been to blurt out info on the supernatural event that had transpired earlier this evening.

"How do you know that Mazie...never mind." I was going to question *how* my mother had known of a witch's death when she'd given up the life of witchcraft, but it was best I didn't know all of her secrets. I'd come to find that I dealt better with small doses of the mystical happenings than a full-on leap off the cliff. "Mazie informed Leo and I that her familiar hadn't crossed over to the other side with her. She came to us seeking assistance, but Eileen walked in on our encounter and scared Mazie off. We haven't seen her since."

A quick glance at the cottage revealed that Leo had beat me home, as usual.

He was currently lying on his back puffing away on his pipe. He had a pillow under his head, lying in full view of one of the front windows without a care in the world, which indicated to me that all was normal in the house.

Apparently, no unwelcome visitors from the other side and no unexpected trouble had landed on our doorstep...currently covered in a light dusting of snow.

I always keep a few lights on inside and out since we usually got home after dark. Unfortunately, the golden hues from the bulbs gave off an eerie ambiance and an even more sinister look as the menacing darkness seemed to swallow the radiating beams.

Think of a stereotypical haunted house at the edge of town in any horror movie you've ever seen. Yeah, that pretty much summed up the exterior of where I live. The tangled overgrowth that had taken over the edges of the cottage had lost its leaves, as well as the two ancient oak trees on either side of the sidewalk leading up to the front door. For some reason, the darkness of the bark glistened even more ominously with the addition of wet snow.

Don't let the spooky description fool you, though. The interior was absolutely stunning, and the massive inland lake which was fed by the bay behind the property made this piece of land prime realty.

"Listen to me very carefully," my mother cautioned, dropping her voice as if someone might overhear her. It was hard to ward away the shiver of fear that had washed over me. The only explanation as to why she'd lowered her tone in such an ill-omened manner was that she wasn't alone. I'd thought she'd be home this late at night, but maybe that wasn't the case. "You need to burn some sage in every corner of the house and tea shop, as well as sprinkle some sage over three fresh hardwood logs in your fireplace for good measure. Light the fire and make sure it burns through the witching hour. One can never be too careful or burn too much sage in situations like these."

I could just picture my mother rubbing her fingers together to mimic the gesture of sprinkling sage over a piece of wood. She'd never want to hear it, but the Marigolds *did* somewhat resemble witches. We all had black hair, green eyes, and porcelain skin with a propensity to wear red nails and matching lipsticks. Well, Nan and my mother wore red lipstick. I liked mine to be more a brownish red so that the sight of me wasn't such a jolt to one's senses upon our first casual introduction.

I'm getting sidetracked again.

Anyway, I'd kept my Corolla running to keep the interior heated, though I had put the gear into park. Since we'd taken a break so I could describe my family's features, now was also probably a good time to explain that my mother's name was Regina.

You see, all the women in the Marigold family had a name that began with the letter R. Oh, and we all had Lattice as a middle name. I was still attempting to go through the boxes Nan had left behind in the bedroom loft, but there was only so much time in any given day. According to Leo, I also had a required reading list somewhere in that mess.

"I mentioned sage to Leo, but he wasn't too convinced it would work." After I'd dropped the bombshell about wanting an assistant to finagle some more time off to improve my quality of life here in Paramour Bay, Leo had been a tad bit irritated. I didn't understand what the big deal was with me bringing in part-time help at the tea shop, but he'd already moved on to explain that sage only kept *evil* spirits at bay...not spirits of witches, per se. "Something about using sage only for malevolent spirits."

"Leo has forgotten that fairies fall under that title," Regina said rather wryly, apparently having the same opinion of fairies as Leo. "A bit of sage should keep Mazie away, though I do find it odd that Strifle didn't join her on the other side as is the usual practice. Not enough for you to go poking your nose into the coven's business, mind you. They have a habit of looking back at anyone with the temerity to involve themselves in coven business even if you had just cause...which you don't."

"You know Strifle?" I asked in surprise, taking off my gloves so that I could put my hands in front of the vent. The steady heat was enough to cause goosebumps up and down my arms, but in a good way. I couldn't wait to get inside to enjoy a cup of hot coffee in front of the fireplace. "Is she like Tinkerbell? And what do you mean by the coven's business?"

"I met Mazie a time or two when I was a young girl, but that was when your grandmother still had a few lingering ties to the coven." My mother paused, which told me she was carefully selecting her words. My interest piqued even more. Nan and my Aunt Rowena had stopped speaking many years ago due to an argument over a man—supposedly around the time that my grandmother was pregnant with my mother. It was also around the same time Nan had been formally excommunicated from the coven I'd never met, all because she'd gotten personally involved with someone outside of the coven's purview. "Mazie and Strifle were definitely a handful, but strict adherence to the coven rules kept them in line. Who knows what trouble Mazie is capable of now that she's crossed over?"

Had someone thought this through along the same lines as my mother? Was Strifle purposefully being kept from following Mazie to the other side? Or was Mazie right in her accusation that the council members were the ones to abduct Strifle?

Regardless of the mischief the two might have concocted on this earth, it wasn't fair for anyone to keep the two of them apart now that they'd done their penance here on this side. My situation had been different. Nan had purposefully bribed Leo to stay behind to help me transition, and I'd grown so attached to him in such a short time.

Sure, Leo could be a pain in my tush, but he'd say the same about me. I couldn't help but smile, knowing full well that we found companionship by being in each other's lives in spite of our stubbornness.

There *was* something that I didn't understand, and I'd love some clarification while I had my mom on the line.

"Speaking of the coven, is there a reason no one has reached out to me yet?" I didn't want to come across as being hurt over the perceived slight, but that was rather hard to do when I didn't know the reason they were shunning me. I mean, you'd think the council would want to welcome a brand-new witch who'd just come into her powers, regardless to whom she was related. Then again, I *had* broken one of their main rules for behavior two months in by telling an ordinary human about the supernatural realm. On top of that, I was dating a man quite prominent in the community who didn't have any ties to the supernatural. I guess I could see the coven's point in ignoring my existence. "Is it because I told Heidi or that I had a date with Liam after coming into my powers?"

"No, dear. The Marigold history with the coven goes way

back, though your Aunt Rowena remained with them after your grandmother moved to Paramour Bay. They have kept their distance ever since." My mother muffled the phone with her hand. It was obvious that she was talking with someone, and I wondered if whoever it was had to do with that lunch date she'd had a while ago. "You never value my opinion, Raven, but at least trust your grandmother's judgment. She made a life for herself outside of the council's reach and its other witches, and I suggest you do the same. Stay far away from them."

"It's not like I know who they are to even reach out to if I wanted," I said dryly, turning down the heat and reaching for the passenger side seat to grab my purse. That cup of coffee had been sounding good all day, but now I was craving the caffeine within the rich beverage. It was a good thing I was one of the lucky ones who could absorb caffeine in copious amounts without it affecting my sleep cycle. "Don't worry, Mom. I also have no desire to be at the beck and call of wayward witches and their affairs, so I'll make sure to burn the sage tonight. Hey, where are you, anyway?"

The long pause was conspicuous, and it didn't surprise me when my mother pulled one of her standard getaway cards.

"What's that, dear? It seems we're getting some bad reception. We'll talk tomorrow. Don't forget about the sage over three fresh hardwood logs!"

With that last directive, my mother disconnected our call without a by your leave. This bad avoidance habit of hers had started the day I'd moved to Paramour Bay. Granted, she'd stopped bugging me about moving back to New York City, but I had no doubt she hadn't given up on that objective quite yet.

It didn't take me long to kill the ignition, tighten my scarf, and pull on the door handle. I'd braced myself for the cold, but one never really prepared themselves enough for that biting wind coming off the lake. Seeing as the front door was no more than forty feet away, it was pointless for me to put my gloves back on.

I grabbed the freezing latch on the wrought iron gate, not surprised when the squeak alerted anyone within a half mile radius that it had been opened—not that anyone was that close to the property. Nan's cottage had been built on the edge of town, but I'm relatively certain she'd done so on purpose to keep prying eyes away.

Curiously, Leo was no longer parked on his pillow in the window.

I very briskly made my way down the sidewalk before sliding my key into the keyhole, but the deadbolt had already been turned. The door had already been unlocked, which was rather unusual.

I know what you're thinking, but it wasn't an intruder and it certainly wasn't Mazie Rose Young.

"Hey, guys," I called out happily, stomping my feet on the slab of rock before stepping inside. It was good to be home. The warmth enveloped me, and I was tinkled pink to see that a fire had already been made in the hearth. "Leo, you'll be happy to know that Mom said sage will work on Mazie and Strifle. And as for you, Ted, I was able to order the suit today that you liked so much online."

I don't know why you keep ordering him suits. Have you seen the man's closet?

"What is Mr. Leo complaining about now?"

"Nothing you need to worry about, Ted," I responded, frowning to let Leo know that it wasn't nice to be rude. I set my purse down on the entry table next to the antique coatrack. There used to be a beautiful bowl I set my keys in, but Leo had

37

KENNEDY LAYNE

broken it last month with his normal casual disregard for anyone else's possession besides his own. In its place was a wooden bowl that I'd found in the cabinet that held pestles and mortars instead of the usual china found in most homes. "Your new suit will be here by the end of the week."

"Thank you, Miss Raven."

Go ahead. Tell the reader what Ted is so that we can get the usual shock and awe routine out of the way. We have sage to burn and spells to cast, and we shouldn't waste another minute on sentiments, which are lost on Ted anyway.

Okay.

So, most of you know what Ted is, but for those of you who are visiting Paramour Bay for the first time…well, let's just say that once upon a time I thought Ted might be an actual zombie.

Don't worry, he isn't.

But…I'll insert the drumroll here.

Ted is technically a wax figure brought to life.

There's no "technically" about it. He used to be made of wax, now he's a mystical automaton. I'm pretty sure Rosemary opted for the bargain basement model with half a brain. Go ahead, ask him if he brought sage with him tonight.

"Ted, did you bring sage?"

"Of course," Ted answered as he slid the fire poker back into its stand.

I'll make this quick. You see, Nan mixed a golem enchantment with some form of an anthropomorphism incantation. It's a mouthful, I know. Anyway, she'd done so once before with terrible ramifications, but she'd learned to tweak the spell so that no one questioned Ted's identity.

Ted is basically Lurch from "The Addams Family" without the sense of humor. Where did he put the sage?

38

Leo was scratching through a basket of herbs that Ted had brought with him this evening, as he does every day. I have no idea where he obtains such rare ingredients such as Galangal Root, Devi's Shoestring, and Kava Kava to name a few, but I'd found it was better not to ask certain questions if I didn't need to know.

You might want to let them know that Ted lives in the back-yard shed. It's not every day that a homeowner has a six-feet, six-inch giant with a couple broken teeth as a caretaker.

What Leo is trying to tell you is that there's a small house—

Shed.

Fine. There's a rather small shed in the backyard where Ted lives.

There's no sage in here, Raven. No sage at all. I'm trying to keep myself together here.

"What is Mr. Leo carrying on about now?" Ted asked, his words a bit stilted.

It was par for the course, and something that I'd gotten used to since meeting him. Unfortunately, he wasn't a witch, so therefore he couldn't hear Leo. I usually ended up translating his meows and strangled noises so that everyone was on the same page.

There won't be another page to be had if we don't burn some sage!

"Leo is searching for sage. He thought you might have brought it in the batch of ingredients this evening." I managed to get my dress coat off and hung up on the antique coat rack, as well as exchanging my favorite pair of knee high boots for my fuzzy slippers. "Are you ready for this, Ted?"

"I'm not sure," Ted answered in his usual formal and succinct manner.

Leo continued to search inside the basket as I made my way

across the hardwood floor. I know I mentioned that the interior of the cottage was stunning, but my words didn't do it justice.

Nan had the best taste when it came to design, whether it be in clothes, jewelry, or the inside of a home. The modern décor, sprinkled with exquisite antique furniture, was something off the front page of *Better Homes & Gardens*. Anyone who managed to get by the appearance of the outside was equally as surprised by the interior.

Are we really talking about interior design when we might be under attack by a spirit looking for a fairy? They're vicious little buggers, Raven. Just vicious!

Ted tugged on his lapels, as if he were bracing himself for some bad news. Leo's frantic digging became even more so, but it was better to let him exhaust himself out than try to reason with him at a time like this.

Technically, it was a quick fix...at least according to my mother.

Anyway, that vintage china cabinet I was telling you about was to my right, along with a matching dining room table. To the left of me was the living room furniture, made of a beautiful cream-colored microfiber material that Leo couldn't ruin with his claws. The kitchen was ahead of me, with every modern appliance you could think of and a small island with stools that were just the right height. The bedroom loft was visible above, accessed by the spiral staircase near the bathroom on the right-hand side of the room.

My sights were focused on the coffeemaker that sat next to the stove, and I made a beeline for the essential machine that brewed the most delicious beverage in the world.

I know, I own a tea shop.

Sue me.

"We were visited by a bona fide, honest to goodness ghost at the shop this evening!"

A part of me was actually pretty excited now that the shock had worn off. I quickly shuffled across the dark hardwood floor to get started on the coffee, needing a cup to warm me up after having come in from the cold.

"Her name was Mazie Rose Young. Get this, Ted. She said we were the talk of the afterlife! Can you believe that? I was getting ready to close up shop, so I walked to the back room to grab my dress coat, reentered the main shop...and lo and behold, she was sitting at one of the high-top tables drinking a cup of tea as if it was the most normal thing in the world for a ghost to be doing. It was absolutely crazy! She purposefully sought us out to figure out why her familiar didn't cross to the other side when it was both their times to go, and it was then that Leo remembered..."

My voice slowly trailed off after I turned around and realized I had been left talking to myself once again. Ted was nowhere to be found. He'd simply left the house without a word as per his usual MO.

Leo was still fiercely digging through the various roots and herbs as if looking for world salvation. Tidbits, fragments, and dried up verdures were going this way and that in Leo's attempt to locate the sage.

No time for stories, Raven! Ted went to get more sage, though he swears he packed some in this basket. Grab the lighter and get ready to—

The sudden drop in temperature had me abruptly stopping midstride to help Leo find the sage so that he could calm down a bit, but I might have been too lax in accepting his insistence that we should hurry in that endeavor. The chilled air hadn't come before Mazie's previous visit, but after. What was so different now?

"Um, Leo?" I cautiously looked around for any sign of Mazie, but she never appeared. That sinking feeling when trouble was near had definitely settled in my stomach, but the palm of my hand remained cool. Did that mean Mazie couldn't cross over the veil that existed between us? Then again, the sensation in my hand hadn't alerted me to her presence the first time around. "I don't think Mazie has enough energy for another visit quite so soon."

You'd be wrong.

Sure enough, Mazie began to slowly materialize on one of the stools at the counter—two feet from where I was standing. The tea cup and matching saucer she'd brought with her the first time around were positioned in front of her, and she was wearing the same floral print dress with the pink floppy hat as before.

There was only one difference, and I couldn't prevent my eyes from widening in shock—Mazie wasn't alone this time around.

Five

───────

"Raven, I'd like for you to meet Lucille Rebecca Barnes," Mazie said with delight. She leaned forward and covered her pearls with her fingers as she shared what seemed to be a secret. "Lucy and your great-great-great-grandmother go back more years than you can count."

"I just had to meet the infamous Raven Lattice Marigold!" Lucy exclaimed from her standing position next to the counter. My gaze darted down to her feet, but I could barely make out anything below where her knees should have been. She was dressed very conservatively in a grey buttoned down cotton dress from a bygone era. She was in total contrast to Mazie's bright presence. The only thing the two had in common were their wide smiles. "Your family on the other side are ecstatic you've finally found your calling."

Leo's continued silence was rather alarming.

Mazie and Lucille's unexpected visit had Leo scrambling off the coffee table, which by far was my favorite piece of furniture in the room. It could do without any more scratches from Leo's claws, but I couldn't even be mad at him for potentially leaving more marks on the surface, because the panic he was currently experiencing had made its way to me.

The roots, herbs, and rose petals that Ted had so meticulously collected and segregated inside the basket were now scattered everywhere in Leo's attempt to flee. He seemed to have momentarily forgotten that he could disappear at will.

"Mazie, I—"

"Let me have my say first, Raven. My time is limited. Earlier, we were interrupted before I could reply to Mr. Leo's description of my character. You see, I wanted to come back and clarify a few things before you start your search for Strifle," Mazie explained as Lucille patted the tea drinking spirit on the shoulder. Both apparitions looked over their shoulders to where Leo now sat ramrod straight next to the front door, his larger left eye glued to our visitors. "I might enjoy a good trick every now and then, but I'm not intentionally cruel. Life should be enjoyed, my dear, not endured. Every day should count for something learned or loved, and laughter should be had either way. That's how I lived my life, and that's how I intend to carry on in my existence beyond the veil."

I love hearing my proper title, but not enough to throw myself into a headlong search for a fairy. Raven, send them on their way, please.

Leo had regained his composure, allowing me to breathe a little easier. My coffeemaker was beeping, but I didn't make a move toward the other side of the kitchen. I had a feeling I was going to need something stronger than coffee to get me through the entirety of this evening.

"You don't believe you can rest in the afterlife without Strifle," I said after clearing my throat a couple of times to make sure I sounded as if I had some measure of self-control. This ghost thing had a way of rattling a person right down to their socks. "Mazie, I'm...honored that you think I can help you."

Good start. Good start.

"And Lucille, it's always nice to meet a dear friend of a relative who died long before I was born," I tacked on, not wanting to offend the other apparition with her tenuous ties to my family. It was rather unsettling to know that spirits could make an appearance anytime they wanted to, and also offensive that Nan hadn't thought to pay me a visit as of yet. I'd have to think on that bit of knowledge later...after all the sage Ted could find was burning in every corner of the cottage. "Unfortunately, I'm not the witch to help you solve your mystery. My suggestion would be to call on one of the witches who are in good standing within the coven, who have better access to the individuals who would have likely had the ability to keep your familiar from crossing over into the afterlife."

Well done, Raven! Wait. Why aren't they fading away?

Silence had descended, though I wasn't sure it was because of my little speech or the fact that Mazie was taking another sip of her tea. Lucille sat there staring at me as if I was the one who'd surprised her with a visit.

Where was Ted with more of that sage?

Good question. I'll go find out. Stay safe.

And just like that, Leo vanished into thin air. He'd left me to deal with two spirits on my own, and I had no choice but to wait until he came back with the sage.

"You are precisely who I need to help find my itty-bitty Strifle," Mazie announced, carefully setting down her tea cup as if it could shatter with the slightest impact. I was pretty sure she had nothing to worry about there, but maybe old habits die hard. I winced at the pun. "I'm certain my passing occurred due to natural causes, but toward the end of my existence in the living realm...let's just say the coven was in somewhat of a disarray. Simply put, I don't trust anyone associated with the coven to handle this tragedy properly. Between you and me, I'm pretty sure the gold-digger is responsible for abducting Strifle."

Lucille had stopped smiling.

Have you ever seen an unhappy non-smiling ghost?

It was downright creepy enough that I took two steps back.

"Lucille, don't do that," Mazie chastised with a flick of her wrist. "You're only here because I needed your energy after my first visit depleted mine. The gatekeeper won't be happy to find that you used your ticket to upset the balance of things. Remember, Karma takes care of these things for us. It wouldn't do to tempt fate."

Ticket? Karma?

I didn't tell you about the ticket system? It's quite simple, really. All spirits who have passed through the veil need a very valid reason to come back to the earthly plane before they're granted visitation tickets.

Leo was finally back, and his words reassured me until I gave it some thought. Only spirits who have passed through the veil? What about the ones who hadn't?

Of course, Leo confirmed my suspicions before I could even part my lips.

It's only the troubled spirits who haven't passed through the veil that you have to worry about.

"Oh, yes!" Mazie agreed with Leo, nodding her head up and down to the point that her floppy hat rippled in time with her movements. "Mr. Leo has a point there. Stay away from those pesky troubled souls who haven't transitioned. Is that why you needed the sage?"

Given that I was currently speaking to two ghosts who

were being rather pesky themselves, I wasn't sure how to reply. I didn't have to when the sound of the front door opening caught our attention.

It seemed that Ted had finally joined us.

Think again.

Sure enough, Ted's pale hand and black sleeve gradually inched through the slit and dropped a bunch of sage on the ground before ever so slowly retreating back out and closing the door.

Chicken.

"Isn't that calling the kettle black?" I muttered, not so sure having Mazie see what he'd brought me was such a good idea, but it was too late. One, she'd already heard me and Leo talking about it. Two, it was evident when she finally realized that it had been brought to burn because of her. "We were just being overly cautious. Right, Leo?"

We were caught red-handed. No use denying it, kiddo.

On the bright side, at least I understood why Nan hadn't been able to join Mazie.

From Lucille's apparel and the fact that she'd known my great-great-great-grandmother, she'd passed on many, many years ago. She had the ability to muster enough energy to assist Mazie, but Nan might not have had enough to come through clearly. And Nan would never have been given a ticket by the gatekeeper for a simple, single visit of her own.

"I'm deeply hurt, Raven," Mazie declared with a frown after watching Ted attempt to sneak the sage through the door. She patted her hand against her chest as if I'd broken her heart. Her reaction was enough to get me to step forward, but not enough for me to reach out to her. "I have no one else to turn to! Isn't that right, Lucille? Raven, you're my last hope. It's not like I can pay a visit to the council when I believe they are the ones who stole Strifle to begin with!"

Lucille nodded her head in sympathy and rested a comforting hand on Mazie's shoulder.

Don't do it, Leo warned, the tufts of orange and black fur on his back standing to attention. *Don't fall for their guilt trip!*

"What is it that you think I can do?" I asked, wondering if there was something I was missing in the bigger picture. "I have no connection to the coven, no idea of who is even in the coven, and I don't even know where the coven is located in order to talk with anyone about Strifle."

I concur. Raven does not possess that type of required information, so all would be for naught.

Leo's confirmation was met with him vanishing from the door and reappearing on the counter with a squint of his vivid green eyes.

You may now be on your way. Sorry for your loss.

Leo had apparently found some courage in the face of these two spirits, and it was nice to have a bit of backup against the unknown. I couldn't help but cross my arms to give the appearance that we were on the same page, but I also wanted to let them down gently.

There was something very endearing about a tea drinking ghost and her supportive friend. Would Heidi and I be the same way in the afterlife?

"Mazie, helping to solve a few small mysteries here in the town of Paramour Bay is one thing." I ignored Leo's twitching whiskers as I attempted to explain our reasoning for not helping them. After all, they were both sweet old ladies who'd passed on to the other side and not one of those ill-omened spirits who had an agenda. At least, I think I was reading the situation correctly. "I know almost everyone in town, and it's easy for me to talk to the residents without causing undue attention to my secret life as a witch. You can see how my not having even a casual connection to the coven would make it nearly impossible for me to find the answers you're seeking."

Well said, Raven. Well said. The last meeting of the Dead Shouldn't Be Hanging Around Here Society *is officially adjourned. Good day to you, ladies.*

Lucille's rather haunting eyes focused on Leo. He wisely scooted back an inch using his front paws to push himself up, his left eye contracting in response to Lucille's intimidation.

"Don't you see why your nonexistent link to the coven is exactly the reason why you're the perfect witch to find my Strifle?" Mazie gushed, causing Lucille to nod once more in agreement. I was definitely somehow losing ground, and it was rather frightening at how good these spirts were at manipulation. I couldn't imagine dealing with an angry one who refused to see reason. "You now have a practical motive to introduce yourself by extending condolences on my passing. You could seek to reconcile yourself with the coven and conduct your investigation as a postulant. Before you enter the coven's inner sanctum, you can cast a truth enchantment. Whoever the guilty party is will confess to their crimes without a thought of deception. You'll be able to free Strifle from whatever horrible curse that has been cast to trap her, and you'll be able to reject becoming an acolyte based on their corruption of the coven's covenant. They'll have no choice but to allow you to leave the maternal order to come home free of their bindings while the council faces their punishment. It's absolutely perfect!"

No, it's not. Where is she getting this horse pucky? Has she snuck a puff of my catnip? That's clearly the worst idea I've ever heard, and I've had to listen to you on a daily basis.

Mazie was still clapping her hands in excitement, purposefully ignoring Leo's rant.

I mean, it's really a bad idea, Raven—right up there with hugging bear cubs in the wild. You can see that, right?

"I'm in agreement with Leo," I responded warily, comprehending the difficult situation we'd now been placed in. "I'm what you might call a bit accident prone with my casting...in general. I'm still learning the nuances, and you're asking me to go up against a well-organized group of seasoned witches—possibly with more than one involved in the kidnapping if your claims against the council is true—who would most likely harm me in unimaginable ways."

Oh, they wouldn't do that to one of their own. They actually have quite the imagination, that sort does. They'd just turn you into a toad or a goat. Maybe they'd even draw your mother into their revenge.

I didn't get a chance to ask Leo if he was being truthful or just trying to scare me into getting rid of Mazie and Lucille faster than their current course of departure. Lucille spoke her final declaration, which had me completely teetering on the edge of what I'd thought was my final decision.

"Strife is in pain, Raven. No matter the spell they've used to bind her here, it would have a vicious effect on her." Lucille's plea had me beginning to think she wasn't so bad. "She needs your help."

Oh, that was a low blow. Minus one point for hitting below the belt.

"Strife is in pain?" I asked, this time forgetting my fear and lowering my arms so that my hands rested on the island. "How do you know?"

We're losing ground, aren't we? This is not going the way I'd planned. You've got to snap out of it!

"It is extremely painful anytime a familiar is separated from their host against their will," Mazie responded as she clutched her handkerchief in grief. "You should know that Mr. Leo. My poor Strifle. Please, Raven. I'm begging you to find my precious familiar and release her from whatever dark spell the culprit has used to bind her."

I was quite torn on how to answer, because my reasoning on why it wasn't a good idea was sound. Why was I hesitating?

Your reasoning was very sound, right up to the point that your head got in the way.

Nothing had changed.

Hollow, I swear.

"Leo, Nan had you remain here for a reason. You agreed to that arrangement, and yet you suffered certain consequences," I reminded him gently, clutching my fingers into the palms of my hands. "How much pain are we talking about? Physical? Emotional?"

They're playing on your sympathies, of which I'll remind you that I have very little. You're going to cave and burn the both of us, aren't you? You're going to end up a member of the very small coven your grandmother fought to abandon, and I'll be right there with you suffering the lot. Congratulations. I've failed in every duty Rosemary left for me to accomplish.

I wasn't sure how I could help Mazie, but it was clear that neither Leo or I could allow a familiar to be in eternal pain by not being allowed to cross into the afterlife. Mazie and Lucille were both staring at me with hopeful expressions, not even bothering to answer my previous question.

We're both such suckers, but your mother will blame me.

"You should know that I still believe someone on the council is involved with preventing Strifle from being with me," Mazie said, now that she could obviously see us caving in under the pressure. There was a slight flicker to their bodily forms. "Whoops! I'm on limited time, Raven, so listen closely. The council consists of the warlock, the gold-digger, the redhead, and the clueless one. I'd lean toward the gold-digger, if I were you. Something on this side is telling me it's one of them, so that's where you should start."

That doesn't sound right. That's not the council I remember.

"Fine, Mazie." I signed in resignation, wondering how much yelling I was going to have to endure from my mother and how she was going to react to my decision to seek out the coven that had all but banned the Marigolds from their midst. "I'm not promising anything, but I will look into who prevented Strifle from crossing over and entering the afterlife with you. Four suspects? That's better than an entire town, so it shouldn't too hard. Right?"

Mazie and Lucille celebrated while Leo and I looked at one another with a combined sense of pessimistic resignation.

Five chances out of ten that your mother passes out dead away. As for the two of us, I can see our future as clear as day. Can you, Raven? We're marching ourselves right into the clutches of the coven. Death awaits us. I always knew a fairy would be my downfall...or a spider.

Six

You can blame Rosemary. She's dead, and she won't complain.

I turned the open sign over so that my customers would see that the tea shop was ready for business, shaking my head at Leo's attempt at changing the subject.

What? Too soon?

It was exactly eight o'clock in the morning, and I was trying to prepare myself for the inevitable phone call to my mother. She was the only one who had the vital information I needed to start my search for Strifle.

"The black magic's side effects should only have affected your short-term memory, Leo," I explained, having read through the spell that Nan had used to keep her familiar from crossing into the afterlife with her.

You see, part of the magic used to attract a familiar in the first place comes into play, a result of which was that each shared a certain amount of their life force with their companion from that point on. In effect, the familiar and the witch or warlock were linked physically. One's constitution would be adversely affected by the loss of his or her familiar. Conversely, the loss of a magic user would normally flat out kill any lesser form.

Of course, there were a few cases where a familiar survived the passing of his or her host. However, those were strictly due to the size and virility of the beast in question. A minotaur's constitution far outweighed that of a mere human, regardless of the fact its host had magical abilities.

When Nan passed beyond the veil, the life force she'd left behind in Leo was corrupted and twisted. Basically, their union had been severed by the necromancy spell that prevented Leo's life force from being overwhelmed and causing his death. The ingredients she'd had to use to make its effect permanent would definitely have disturbed his short-term memory and damaged his recall.

"If your long-term memory wasn't supposed to be affected by the material components, maybe I can heal some of the damage caused by the dark nature of the incantation, enabling you to recover from some of the lasting effects."

Have you forgotten what happened on your first attempt at Otis' arthritis antidote? I still have tingling in certain places I shouldn't. Thankfully, it hasn't affected my desire for catnip.

"It was your tail," I replied wryly, amazed at Leo's flair for the dramatic. "My word, you've become quite a scaredy-cat when it comes to intestinal fortitude and possessing a sense of adventure."

The way my morning was starting out, I was grateful that I'd thought to bring double my normal ration of coffee with me from the house. Granted, my all-time favorite beverage was currently residing in a petite teacup with pretty flowers and a unique octagon shape, but the packaging didn't matter as much as the sanity enclosed therein. It wouldn't do for my customers to discover that I preferred coffee over tea.

It was best to maintain the illusion, at least until I expanded the shop's inventory to include gourmet blends of whole bean coffees and the associated machines to grind and brew them. Some of my specialty remedies might be better suited for a robust coffee blend than a less hearty tea.

Ingredients for certain spells could leave a bitter or stronger aftertaste based on their material components, which weren't entirely consumed by the magic. Other times, the spell was cast on the tea itself, and the magical energy had no effect on the taste whatsoever.

"That mishap was quite a while ago, so you can stop bringing it up already."

Never. I felt wounded to my very core.

I enjoyed a sip of my coffee as I watched Eileen get out of her car all bundled up like we'd experience the snow-apocalypse. In her defense, it was chilly outside, but she was wearing new earmuffs that utilized more fur on them than Leo's entire coat. I waved back when she caught sight of me staring.

Eugene and Albert, the two older gentlemen who played chess every day over at Monty's hardware store, were both entering Trixie's Diner for their morning breakfast. It was a known fact that they ate the same dish each day. They said it was hearty enough to stick to the ribs of a veteran lumberjack. Their daily breakfast consisted of a bed of shredded fried potatoes, covered with a layer of scrambled eggs before being smothered in sausage gravy. They scooped it all up with an order of toasted sourdough bread before washing it down with a full pot of black coffee.

I surmised early on that their life expectancy as a direct result of such a meal would be adversely affected. The breakfast might stick to their ribs, but I was fairly sure it would stick to their arteries, as well. Watching them from my warm spot in the tea shop, they appeared to be bantering over something, but they were all smiles this morning.

I'd be smiling too if I didn't have to face an entire coven of witches who'd previously excommunicated our family. By the way, have you thought of what's going to happen when they find out that Rosemary dabbled in black magic and I'm still around?

"One, the council can't re-excommunicate Nan." I didn't think that was an actual word, but Leo got my drift. "Two, as you said earlier—she's dead and won't complain. Nothing will happen."

I should be so lucky. You'll be changing your tune once they notice me.

"Stop that," I chastised, frowning at the fact that Leo would even say something so horrible. "Life isn't something to be taken for granted. Of that, I'm sure Nan would agree."

I suppose it could be worse. That premium organic catnip I ordered online was the bomb. It was easily worth the two hours it took for me to enter your credit card information on the website. It's difficult to type with paws, you know.

I overlooked his obvious ploy to bait me and took another sip of my coffee, relishing the warmth that invaded my body as the caffeine began to course through my veins. I could understand Leo's addiction to smoking his catnip, given my love of the rich beverage.

Standing at the glass door for a few minutes after flipping the sign over had become sort of a ritual for the two of us—Leo in the window on his pillow and me blocking the entrance staring out into the heart of Paramour Bay. River Bay, the main thoroughfare in town, was just beginning to come alive. It was a delight to watch as everyone commenced the start of their day.

The door to the diner opened once more, reminding me that the owner—Trixie— was in her seventies. She didn't actually still cook, but she did make it into the diner every day to oversee the kitchen staff and socialize with the clientele. Trixie was a force to be reckoned with, and I didn't see her joining Mazie on the other side anytime soon.

Larry Butterball was exiting the diner, keeping the door open with his dress shoe for Otis. After an exchange of pleasantries, Larry crossed the street with his briefcase in one hand and his usual cup carrier in the other. Two cups of coffee had been arranged in the tray diagonal from one another to distribute the weight evenly. The ends of his winter scarf carried in the wind behind him as he made his way toward Mindy's boutique. It was wonderful to see the excitement in his eyes as his gaze focused solely on his destination—the shop two doors down from mine. The two of them deserved happiness.

The fact that Leo had been relatively quiet upon my reflection of the townsfolk had me glancing over at him with curiosity. Sure enough, he wasn't in his usual spot near the display window, as I'd thought. I'd even fluffed the soft pillow for him this morning. I'd hoped to shake off the cold due to the glass becoming a bit frosty in the winter months.

"Leo?"

No answer.

I wondered where he'd gotten off to.

Well, now was as good a time as any to call my mother.

Hmmm, not even the mere mention of Regina had Leo scurrying back to tell me that it was a bad idea to involve her. Unfortunately, she was the only one who might have the names of the witches associated with the coven's welcome wagon. I'd asked Ted late last night when he'd came back to retrieve his basket, but he hadn't met any of the witches in the coven, either.

It made me wonder if Nan's creating Ted wasn't against one of the coven's rules, as well. I doubt that his creation would have aided in the council giving Nan any type of forgiveness.

My cell phone began to chime in my purse, so I quickly made my way to the checkout counter. I set down my coffee next to the cash register so that I could dig my phone out from the endless void that was my everyday purse.

Surprisingly...or not so surprising...it was my mother's name appearing on the lighted display.

"Mom? I was just going to call you."

"Whatever it is that's sending rather cagey energy waves my way, you can stop it right now," Regina declared, all but telling me that Leo was the culprit. "You burned the sage that I told you to last night, didn't you?"

"About that," I began, leaning my forearms on the counter as I continued to look out the display window. Tuesday mornings were fairly quiet, but I spent the entire day yesterday restocking the shelves. I suppose I could rearrange some of the new merchandise I've been meaning to get to in last week's shipment, but I'd probably use this downtime to create a flier to put in the window advertising for my part-time help. "The sage didn't quite work. Mazie and a friend dropped in for a visit before I could burn the sage."

The long pause on the end of the line was expected, but it was drawn out to the point where I wasn't sure if my mother had actually disconnected the call.

"Mom? Are you still there?"

"Please, please, please tell me that you sent Mazie and

whoever she brought with her on their merry way." My mother wasn't that easily rattled, especially when it came to witchcraft and the mystical ways of the magical world. Sure, she didn't want me to have anything to do with our family heritage. She'd been very vocal about her displeasure of my choice, thus far. Regardless, she always came through when I needed her. "Where is Leo? Is he there? Put me on speaker."

It was true that all witches could hear familiars, but too long of a distance put a damper on communications.

"Leo's out making his morning rounds." At least, I was hoping he was just taking a morning stroll through town. Fairies weren't the only ones who liked to stir up trouble. "Mom, Leo agreed that we should attempt to locate Strifle and remove the binding spell. Apparently, it's rather painful for familiars to be separated from their host unwillingly. We couldn't stand by and do nothing, knowing full well that a magical creature was in agony."

"Then recommend to Mazie that she seek out another witch, preferably one familiar with the coven." I could tell from my mom's tone that she hadn't intended the pun about familiars. I also recognized the losing battle ahead, but even she could understand why Leo and I couldn't turn away a spirit in need. "Mazie must know someone who can help her that wouldn't risk upsetting the balance of things as they are now. I was rather young the last time your grandmother and I ran into her, but she seemed to fit in with the other witches just fine."

"That's the thing, Mom. Mazie mentioned that the coven was in a bit of disarray before she passed. She's also pretty confident that someone on the council prevented Strifle from passing over the veil, so at least we know who the suspects are." I reached underneath the counter and pulled out the laptop that Nan had used for business purposes. It was relatively new, purchased within a year of her death, and I didn't see the need to replace it. It took all of two minutes to guess Nan's password —Witch01. "Mazie doesn't know who she can trust, so I was hoping you could give me a list of names of potential witches who might still be with the coven."

Another long pause that I had fully expected.

"Mom, I don't even know where the coven is located. That makes it rather hard for me to look into Strifle's kidnapping, or whatever you want to call it." I took a sip of coffee while the laptop booted up. I was relatively pleased with how this phone conversation was going, considering the alternative. "All I'm asking for is one name of someone who might be able to help me get to the bottom of this. I'll reach out to him or her by phone, if that makes you feel better. I don't have to go anywhere near the coven."

"A phone call only?" my mother asked warily.

"Phone calls only," I promised, though I felt the need to tack on an addendum to that oath. "Unless I can't reach anyone. Then I might have to take a little road trip, but it's not like I can do that in the middle of the week. Heidi mentioned she *might* be able to visit this weekend, so I can promise you that I won't go alone...if it comes to that eventuality."

Maybe I should have left off the addendum.

"Mom?" I decided to hammer in the nail just a bit. "You really don't want me going on social media, asking anyone if they know of a coven that's located in Connecticut, do you? Mazie said there's a warlock, a gold-digger, a redhead, and someone who's rather clueless. That doesn't leave me a lot to go on."

I couldn't help but smile at envisioning Mom's look of horror. I'd never in a million years do something that drastic unless it was a life or death situation. Technically, Strifle's circumstances *were* life and death. Still, I wouldn't resort to that level and risk outing an entire population of witches.

"Merrick Bronach." The name was said after hearing my mother's audible sigh of parental frustration. "Do not, I repeat, do not go see him personally. Phone calls only, but he can provide you with the information you need."

I couldn't understand how my mother was this wealth of information when it came to witchcraft when she'd had nothing to do with the supernatural growing up. By the time Mom was born, Nan had already severed ties with her own sister and the coven.

"I'm surprised that Nan shared all of this information with you, considering your disposition toward the supernatural." The laptop had finally come to life, and I maneuvered the square mousepad until the little arrow on the screen was hovering over the PowerPoint icon. "I was afraid you wouldn't know of anyone who could help."

"You know your grandmother," my mother replied, attempting to smooth over the realization I'd just made. She'd made a major mistake, though. I *hadn't* known Nan that well, and it was all due to my mother's decision to move far away and expunge any use of witchcraft from our lives. "She was a talker, that one."

"No, she wasn't." I straightened my shoulders, deciding that I could handle a few more answers regarding our past history. "Mom, you went behind Nan's back and looked into the coven when you were a teenager, didn't you? What did you find out? Better yet, who did you talk to? It was Merrick Bronach, wasn't it? He talked to you back then, which is why you think he'll talk to me now."

"Raven? I didn't hear your last question." Mom was pulling her usual stunt, but I'd lost any humor at her attempt to evade the topic of discussion. "I think we have a bad connection."

"No, we don't. You're trying to wiggle your way out of telling me what I need to know, just like every time we talk about—"I pulled the phone away from my ear once I realized the line had gone dead.

It figured.

I wasn't going to let my mother ruin a perfectly good day, though.

I'd gotten a name of someone who might be able to help me locate the coven and just possibly Strifle. My to-do list was mounting. I still needed to find part-time help for the tea shop, and I needed to find something to wear for my dinner date this Friday night with Liam. On top of all that, Leo had left me alone long enough to enjoy the rest of my coffee.

Raven!

Apparently, I spoke too soon.

"Yes?" I pulled the stool behind me closer to the counter so that I could sit down while creating an advertisement for part-time help. I'd make it colorful enough to catch someone's eye. "And don't tell me that Ted walked into town this morning after I offered him a ride. He said he was going to stay home today and do inventory on the ingredients I needed for all of the Valentine's Day orders I have lined up for next month."

I was going to try my hand at a love blend, similar to the one that Nan had created for Pearl and Henry. Those two lovebirds had jetted to Florida to escape the cold, and I couldn't be happier that they'd found each other in their early seventies.

Would you stop yammering about hearts and flowers? We have an emergency!

"What emergency?" I asked, finally looking up from the

laptop to find that Leo was pacing back and forth in the display window.

Oh, Leo's angst wasn't a good sign.

I slowly stood from the padded seat, taking time to sense the air around me. Sure enough, there was a low hum of distressed energy vibrating all around us.

Unwelcome visitor incoming! Batten down the hatches! All hands on deck!

Seven

I held my breath as Rye Dolgiram set his hand on the silver handle of the glass door, but he didn't enter. Instead, he paused long enough to pull his cell phone out of his winter jacket. I could see rather than hear that he was receiving an incoming call.

"What on earth could Rye want with me?" I murmured, sitting back down on the stool before my knees gave out in anticipation. "This is strange, Leo, but I don't sense that he's a *danger* here. Do you?"

Something is seriously wrong with that man, Raven. Go lock the door and flip the sign. It's a subtle hint, but I think he'll get the gist. We have enough to worry about in our quest to wrangle a pesky fairy.

I wasn't going to do anything of the sort. Granted, I didn't trust Rye any farther than I could throw him, but I wasn't going to be rude, either. He was a handyman of sorts, doing odds and ends for the businesses and residents alike of Paramour Bay, but there was something very secretive about him that didn't sit right with me.

Gertie, the owner of a New England manor house inn here in town, which was very reminiscent of the Nickels-Sortwell House in Wiscasset, couldn't praise him enough.

Apparently, Rye performed all the maintenance on the old Federal style buildings on her estate. Maybe he was a relative or something, though they didn't look anything alike. He was the epitome of tall, dark, and handsome, whereas Gertie was rather petite and had to have been a blonde back in her heyday, judging from her light complexion. Plus, they had completely different facial features.

Rye stood outside in the cold on the sidewalk talking to someone as if it weren't twenty-some degrees with piercing winds that could cut through three inches of solid steel. Nothing seemed to faze him, not even the fact that both Leo and I were studying him with curiosity. He'd stepped away from the door and shifted so that the gusts weren't hitting him directly from the front.

Rye had to know he had an audience, right? Oddly enough, he lowered his head as if he was consorting with the devil himself before slowly walking away.

You're right. That was strange. I'll follow him and discover all his secrets.

Before I could tell Leo to leave the man alone, he disappeared fast enough to have a few orange and black cat hairs floating in his wake. It *had* been strange the way Rye had decided not to enter the shop, but it was more likely that one of the residents in town had an emergency that couldn't wait to be resolved.

At least, that's what I told myself. Anything else was just wild speculation.

Rye wasn't a tea drinker that I knew of, especially considering he'd never stopped into the shop to buy anything before.

That didn't mean he wasn't used to ordering his supply of richly exotic tea online, but he also struck me as the type of man who drank coffee—strong, black, and scalding hot. He definitely wasn't one of those frou-frou coffee drinkers with the latte crowd.

I guess I'd just have to wait for either Leo to return or Rye to make his way back to the store. I had noticed that there seemed to be a little spark between him and Heidi when they'd first met, though she currently only had eyes for Detective Jack Swanson. In my opinion, she'd chosen wisely this time.

The rest of the morning was spent attempting to concentrate on something else besides the rather peculiar almost-visit by Rye and wondering what Leo was discovering while following the reserved stranger. I didn't like that Leo was being underhanded and snooping around in something that wasn't his business. I mean, what if someone decided to do that to me? They'd find out a lot more than they bargained for, and my life here in Paramour Bay would be over before I could ever utter a word in my own defense.

It was wrong to violate anyone's privacy.

By noon, I'd hung up the flyer I'd created and printed off for part-time help, waited on a couple of my usual customers, and also tried to do an online search for one Merrick Bronach. Unfortunately, the last item on the agenda hadn't panned out so well. Not everyone had an online trail to sniff out, especially folks who avoided technology. As for the gold-digger, redhead, and clueless one...well, it wasn't like I could search those keywords and come up with answers.

I stayed in the tea shop during my lunch hour, not wanting to give up the search for the one person who might be able to figure out why Strifle hadn't crossed over the rainbow bridge with her mistress. There was no indication that anyone by the name of Bronach lived anywhere in the state of Connecticut since before the state had even become a state. It was at least not since the witch trials of the 1600s. There was mention of an Irish Saint in the sixth century, but I dismissed that connection out of hand.

I even widened my search to include other areas, but still to no avail.

I mean, we're talking a general Google search, a social media query on multiple sites, and I was still in the midst of searching for the name my mother had given me when my cell phone chimed at a little after one o'clock in the afternoon.

"Jack just mentioned to me that a man who goes by the name of Beetle is retiring and closing up his accounting firm there in Paramour Bay," Heidi exclaimed in a mixture of excitement and irritation without her standard greeting. She was never one to waste time on anything that didn't have substance, and she always got straight to the point. Living in the huge city of New York City had definitely rubbed off on her demeanor. "Were you intentionally keeping this from me or were you planning on denying me this opportunity out of apathy?"

"I was waiting for when you took a moment to breathe," I corrected her, shoving the laptop back on the counter a bit while I took a break from the endless search of what could possibly be a nonexistent person. My mother wouldn't do that to me, would she? Give me a name to pursue endlessly like Leo chasing his bent tail just to keep me busy while she handled things on her own? I was afraid I already knew the answer to that question. "I know how busy the beginning of the year can be for you, and I didn't want you to think I was putting pressure on you during tax season."

I stood from the stool and stretched my back. Another cup

of coffee sounded wonderful, but I'd already consumed the two cups that I'd brought with me. Maybe I should try the new tea blend that came in on the delivery truck yesterday called Dandelion coffee. The name was definitely attractive, but I hadn't wanted to be disappointed with the taste. My idea to diversify the shop's offerings by including gourmet coffees was becoming more attractive by the day. Maybe I should even start offering hot takeout beverages like a tea and coffee bar from the city.

"So, it's all true? The accountant who takes care of nearly every small business in Paramour Bay is retiring?" Heidi couldn't contain her enthusiasm, which was part of the reason I'd kept quiet. She'd spend every waking hour outside of her current position to try and make this work, all but running herself into the ground. On top of that, I was dealing with a grieving spirit who'd lost her familiar. I was afraid Heidi would attempt to take the rest of the week off. Her loyalties to friends knew no bounds, but I wasn't about to be the reason she was dismissed from one of the top firms in New York City. "Raven, you know how long I've waited for an opportunity like this— an established accounting business of my very own."

"I do, but you should get through these next three months first and leave your employer on good terms. I heard that Beetle isn't going to close his firm until after tax season, anyway, so that gives you time to decide if you truly want to leave behind the Big Apple and all the twinkling lights." I decided now was the time to voice my concern. "My situation was different. I was in a job that was going nowhere, behind on my rent, and looking back...a little lost in every single direction available to me. Nan left me something so much more than a tea shop, Heidi. You said yourself last month that I've created my own little family in the small town of Paramour Bay."

The contemplative quietness that filled the line wasn't the same as my mother's silence. Heidi had heard me, and she was taking my advice to heart.

"I know you have dinner with Liam on Friday night, but maybe I can squeeze some time to take the train out there on Saturday afternoon. I'll stay until late Sunday, and we can go over the pros and cons like true small business entrepreneurs," Heidi suggested, allowing me to breathe a sigh of relief. She was taking this seriously and not jumping in with two feet, the way she usually did with everything in her life. "How is everything there? Did you and Leo get to store all those decorations back into the storage room?"

"Yes, although Leo made it much more difficult by spending all his time chasing the tinsel that I'd strung on that small tree in the corner than he did anything else. Ted was able to stack the boxes in a way that most of them won't come down on my head," I said with a smile, not needing to remind Heidi of my accident-prone tendencies. It also delayed the inevitable decision I'd have to make on whether or not to share the details with her regarding Mazie's visit. "These last two days have been rather slow, but that's only because everyone stocked up before the Christmas holiday. I'm hoping to see a pick up by the end of the month. Then, of course, I have my holistic home remedy business that never slows down."

I couldn't help but glance at the clock behind me. Leo really should have been back by now. If Rye had gone to help someone with a downed tree or something along those lines, wouldn't Leo have left the man to do his business?

"How is everything along that sideline?"

Heidi's vague question told me that she was no longer alone, but she wouldn't disconnect our call until I'd told her that everything was running smoothly on the witchcraft side of things.

It was now or never.

"Good," I answered, choosing not to tell Heidi about my latest side job that entailed finding a familiar in a place I didn't know the location of and a warlock I wasn't even sure existed. Really, what was there to tell? Saying that altogether in my mind made me realize I might not be of any help to Mazie. "Everything's fine."

Being the terrible liar I was, it wasn't a surprise when Heidi suspected I was holding something back. Fortunately for me, I was saved from spilling my guts when someone on her end at the office called her name. She all but promised she'd call me later, but thankfully that wouldn't be until sometime after eight or nine o'clock tonight due to the hours she'd been putting in to keep up with the rush. The reprieve would give me some extra time to decide what, if anything, I could tell her without having her hop a midnight train to Paramour Bay.

The small ding from the laptop told me I'd received an incoming email. You know those sites where you can put a name into a search box, along with any other information you had on an individual? Well, I'd tried that as a last resort. I honestly didn't think I'd get an email back, considering I'd thoroughly searched every nook and cranny of the internet for the last five hours.

I was afraid to click on the message for fear it would tell me that there was no such person by the name of Merrick Bronach.

I need a nap.

My fingers had been hovering over the mousepad embedded in my laptop, but I pulled them away when Leo made his sudden reappearance.

That was exhausting. That man went to the inn, the bakery, Newt's garage, and that was all before he drove into one of those neighborhoods past the courthouse. He's now fixing Wilma's garage door, while both Elsie and Wilma are offering to make him lunch to order.

"So, you're saying that Rye is just a handyman and not some secret axe murderer," I concluded for him, actually pleased to know that Rye was harmless. "Good work, Leo."

I shouldn't be praising Leo for snooping into other people's business, but this tidbit of news was most refreshing. Even my mother had eyed Rye warily when she'd first met him, though that wasn't a surprise. She was usually suspicious of most people on an everyday basis.

Wake me in a few hours when it's time to go home.

Leo plopped his overweight cargo of fur onto the pillow in front of the display window, extending his front legs as he began to get comfortable. I'd put a heating pad underneath the small padded bed so that the cold seeping through the glass pane didn't have Leo catching a cold or worse. His audible sigh of happiness told me he appreciated the kind gesture, even if he didn't say so.

Wait.

Leo's left eyelid popped open, giving me a stare down.

What are you doing on that laptop?

"Mom finally relented and gave me a name of someone in the coven who might be able to help us locate Strifle." I sat back down on the stool and gestured toward the small screen in front of me. "I put the name into a search site earlier, and the company just emailed me back. I had to pay fifty dollars, too."

It wasn't like I was a real private investigator who charged her clients a flat fee and whatever expenses came from the investigation. No, I had to be an amateur witch whose clients were ghosts without means.

"I thought about casting a locator spell, but you weren't here. I didn't—"

I stopped talking when Leo rolled onto his side and pretended he was having a heart attack.

"That's not nice, Leo. I am perfectly capable of casting a simple locator spell, but I didn't have the right ingredients here at the shop." I rolled my eyes when Leo let his tongue hang out from the corner of his mouth. "I'm serious, Leo. Stop. I'm not that bad at casting simple divination spells."

Leo peeked at me, but he could easily see my frustration.

You aren't that bad, but we can discuss that at another time. It's like matching up the local high school football team against the Steelers. You'd have a hard time saying they're playing the same game, now wouldn't you?

Leo managed to shift back onto his somewhat distended stomach and stand on his undersized legs, blinking rapidly as if he were trying to keep himself awake. I figured I only had about three minutes before he collapsed in exhaustion, so I quickly pressed the mousepad.

Well? What did fifty bucks buy you besides repeated solicitations from that website for your next five lifetimes?

"Merrick Bronach *does* in fact exist," I whispered, leaning an elbow on the counter as I delved into the typed information that was apparently worth fifty dollars. "This says that Mr. Bronach is seventy-eight years old and lives in Windsor, Connecticut."

Windsor?

"Is that a problem?" I cast a glance Leo's way, but he'd already moved off of his bed and was making his way toward me. The swish of his tail wasn't so graceful, but more of a tic to show his displeasure. Why? "The town is only an hour from here. Leo, isn't Windsor near Nan's hometown? What was it called? Wethersfield, wasn't it? That rings a bell from earlier."

Jacob Blackleach was from Wethersfield. Get your body count right, Raven.

Ignore Leo. He was just being facetious about how our little side investigative business got started. The first day I'd ever stepped into Paramour Bay was the day I moved my entire life here...only to discover a dead body behind those ivory-colored fairy beads that hid the back room of the tea shop from view.

"They held witch trials in Wethersfield in 1647," I shared from memory, having researched the past of some of my ancestors. I still had a lot of boxes to go through that Nan had left behind, but there was only so much time in the day. "It was the first of that kind of trial in the Colonies. You hear all those stories about Salem and the women they tried there, but they weren't really the first, were they? Come to think of it, all of those witch trials I read about were from around the same, small area near Hartford, just south of Windsor and north of Wethersfield. There must be a link between the coven, our family, and the witch trials."

A spark of excitement ignited within me at the thought of finding out more about my grandmother and our family. There was so much I still didn't know, even after having gone through a few of the boxes that Nan had left behind. Actually, speaking with someone who'd personally known the older generation of Marigolds would be thrilling!

Leo sat back on his haunches, but he refused to jump up on the counter. His green eyes were rather unfocused as he stared off into space, but it was easy to see the tic of his upper whiskers.

It was then I remembered the promise to my mother about

only reaching out to Merrick Bronach by phone. Thinking back on our phone conversation, I realized that I hadn't truly made any such promise.

"Look, it's not that I'm being naïve when it comes to the coven. I understand that they're probably not going to welcome me with open arms, but shouldn't the council be aware that I've come into my powers?" It was a practical question. "Think about it. If those in the afterlife know that we've been using witchcraft to help solve a few mysteries, then it's a reasonable assumption to believe the coven does, too."

It's not the coven I'm worried about. There's a reason your grandmother left Windsor.

"We've already established that you don't like mischievous fairies, but Strifle's abilities are obviously being misappropriated for nefarious reasons. She's being prevented from crossing over to be with Mazie as a consequence." I noticed that Leo didn't seem afraid so much as he was troubled. "If Nan was from Windsor or a small town nearby—and I can't believe I've never known the Marigolds were from that area—then that means Aunt Rowena is probably still living in that town!"

Aunt Rowena's possible presence so close to where I needed to investigate told me everything I needed to know.

"No wonder Mom didn't want us to go see Mr. Bronach in person. Leo, you've had to have known this all along. How did you think we were going to save Strifle without running into Aunt Rowena?"

Magic, Raven. Magic always has a way.

Eight

"Leo, fix what you did to my Corolla right this minute," I harshly demanded so that he didn't misinterpret my anger. "This is not how you resolve a conflict. You can't just use your abilities to deny me the use of my vehicle because you don't like my decision. Besides, someone is going to see me sitting inside this frozen car and decide to come to my rescue. I will then be forced to retaliate by doing something distasteful to you, and I don't want to be that kind of person."

Rescue? Oh, you're thinking of someone like Liam. As you know, he's currently out of town.

I crossed my arms and stomped my feet on the floorboard in hopes to maintain some body heat. I was failing miserably.

"This is so unfair, Leo. Didn't you say we shouldn't use magic for self-gain?"

There were various spells Leo could have used to ensure the engine of my vehicle wouldn't start, so it was pointless for me to try and counteract his incantation. I didn't have enough experience, and I'd only memorized a few by heart over the last couple of weeks. If I was being honest, those spells were only

KENNEDY LAYNE

for when we found ourselves in quite a bit of danger. Should I find myself out here for much longer, this situation would definitely qualify as dangerous.

The good thing about those specific incantations that I'd spent time learning could be used without material components. Instead, I could utilize the energy I was able to pull from my surroundings.

Fairies are exactly the type who could put us smack dab in the middle of trouble. Now, shall we try things my way?

"This is extortion."

This is me being as reasonable as I can manage. You're a witch, Raven. We have the ability to locate that winged urchin without putting our physical bodies in harm's way. You know how much I've grown to love this GQ material bod I'm currently rocking, so give me your word that you'll drive straight home, and I'll let you start the engine.

"We could have been halfway to Windsor by now," I complained as I surveyed the glistening main thoroughfare through town. River Bay was lit on either side by those vintage gas lamp street lights I loved so much, but most of the storeowners had closed their shops at this point. With the dip in temperature, there wasn't a lot of people milling about on the sidewalk without a destination in mind. "Fine. We'll go straight home...for this evening only."

It wouldn't surprise me if we were blessed with another visit from Mazie and Lucille.

Don't jinx us. We don't want to be seen as inviting their company.

"They're probably wondering what's taking us so long to locate Strifle." My words were followed by condensation blowing from lips. I'm not happy I caved, but at least there was warmth in my immediate future. Not wasting another second longer, I leaned forward and turned the key in the ignition. Sure enough, the engine started up beautifully. "I was thinking about Strife this afternoon. What if she couldn't cross through the veil because of a misunderstanding between her and Mazie? You mentioned that fairies are mischievous. What if she's doing this as some sort of trick on Mazie? Maybe she wasn't ready to go."

I did not use the word mischievous. *There are many adjectives I could use to describe those little imps, but mischievous isn't one of them. I'd say malicious...now that would fit the bill.*

"You got tricked by that fairy more than once, didn't you?" I asked with a growing smile, wondering just what Leo had endured by the tiny elf and the fairy dust she could leave behind in her wake as she disappeared. Merrick Bronach wasn't the only individual I'd researched today. Fairies were definitely coveted by some. There was a lot of information about magical fairies on the internet—some of it probably true—which was rather surprising given that humans believed they were mystical creatures. "Oh, come on, Leo. Tell me the truth."

He didn't respond, even after I called his name numerous times.

"Fine," I muttered, turning on my headlights and shifting the gear into drive. Leo would most certainly be lying on his small bed in the front window of home when I pulled up to the wrought iron fence. "Be that way."

Something caught my eye as I started to pull away from the curb. It was Larry, opening the door to Mindy's shop and waiting for her to join him outside. They were both bundled up for the cold weather, and she was locking up her boutique for the evening. It was sweet the way he was watching over her, and I was glad that Mindy had found someone she could enjoy spending time with. She deserved to be happy.

My one and only date with Liam had been the New Year's Eve gala at the wax museum. That story would take too long to tell you due to the mystery involved, but let's just say the evening had ended with a heart fluttering moment—a passionate kiss that I would love to repeat sometime soon. I know you already heard about that part of our date, but it bore repeating.

Anyway, I was really looking forward to this Friday's dinner with Liam. We'd have a chance to finally be alone. Unfortunately, that meant locating Strifle in the next three days and somehow helping her cross to the other side in order to be with Mazie without anyone being the wiser.

Mindy and Larry were waving hello as I drove past, getting ready to make a left on Oceanview Avenue to double back around. I don't know why I didn't park facing the other direction of town where my cottage was located, but either way I was still left with having to do a U-turn. I smiled and waved to the couple who was most likely heading over to the diner for dinner.

My stomach rumbled.

If Leo were still around, I may have been tempted to join Mindy and Larry for dinner. Seeing as my makeshift mentor was waiting for me at home to cast spells I'd never attempted before, it was best I get home before he booby-trapped my car again.

My cell phone rang right as I was pulling up to the cottage. It was most likely my mother checking in on me to make sure I hadn't done anything foolish, like what I'd planned earlier. Honestly, how could I do anything even mildly inappropriate with Leo underfoot twenty-four seven?

I shifted the car into park and left the engine running as I fished my phone out of my purse. Tingles of excitement shot through my gloves as if the vibrations from the cell were plugged into the pads of my fingers. It took me longer than I would have wanted to free up my hand so that I could answer the call.

"Liam, what a nice surprise!"

Was that a too-over-eager response?

"Hello, Raven," Liam responded with a smile to his rich voice. I tilted my head just a bit so that the phone was snugger against my ear. "How is your week going?"

"Pretty slow," I replied, wincing at the fact that I couldn't find anything better to say. He most likely already knew how the town operated after the second week after Christmas. "No one seems to need tea since the holiday. I'm hoping it picks up soon. I put a sign in the window saying I was looking for someone to fill in as part-time help."

Speaking of windows, I glanced toward where Leo usually camped out in the house. He was nowhere to be seen. That alone made me quite anxious, but I wasn't ready to end this phone call just yet.

"I was actually calling to talk about how *you* are doing," Liam corrected me, causing a flush to fill my cheeks. I wasn't the type of woman to get tongue-tied over a man, but this particular male was something special. "Not that I don't want to hear about the shop, but I was calling to check on you."

"Eileen called you about Leo, didn't she?" I asked wryly once I figured out what had truly taken place. It wasn't like I could tell Liam that we'd been visited by a ghost, so I stuck to the story I'd spun for Eileen. "You know that Leo has an overabundance of fur. I mean, he has a very hard time taming those orange and black strands. Anyway, he's been coughing up a lot of...hairballs lately. I was waiting for him to clear his airway when Eileen saw me comforting him."

My story made total sense, right?

I smothered a groan of regret at using another white lie.

This was exactly what a man and woman shouldn't talk about before their second date—hairballs and such. I rested my left cheek against my gloved hand, wondering if anything in my life would ever be normal again.

"I can speak from experience that Dr. Jameson is an excellent vet should Leo need anything," Liam advised, most likely following that piece of sound counsel from Eileen herself. "If you're worried, you could always take Leo in for a checkup or a booster shot."

It hit me that Liam had called out of the blue because he was worried about me. He understood that Leo came with me to the store, sometimes walking with me down the main thoroughfare of River Bay, and he believed that Leo rode in my vehicle back and forth from work to home. Leo had become my rock, my foundation, through this precarious witchcraft journey. Even though Liam didn't understand half of it, he did grasp my love for the snarky rapscallion who constantly overstepped his place.

"Thank you, Liam," I replied softly, his call meaning more to me than he'd probably ever know. "I appreciate the advice regarding Dr. Jameson. It was sweet of you to check in on me."

"I'm looking forward to dinner on Friday." There were a few muffled voices in the background, probably from fellow law enforcement officers. Even though they were probably waiting for Liam, he didn't seem to be in any hurry to disconnect the call. "I hope you like lasagna, because that's the only thing I'm good at making after grilling season is over. I'm a grill master in the summer. I can whip up a pretty good filet, given half a chance."

I couldn't help but smile at the vision of Liam in a red and white checkered apron with a pair of tongs in his hand while standing over a mammoth smoking grill. I'd only ever seen him out of his work element a time or two, but he did allow his playfulness to shine through every now and then—especially when he went to the trouble to sneak me coffee at a random moment during a long workday.

"As a matter of fact, I love lasagna." I would have eaten a starchy piece of paper if it meant spending more time with him. Unfortunately, someone else called his name. "Thanks for checking in with me, Liam."

"I'd like to say I called to solely offer advice on Leo's hair-ball issue, but I was also being a bit selfish. I missed hearing your voice, Raven," Liam revealed, his tone dropping an octave. Either I was having some sort of hot flash or this was what it was truly like to react to a man's overtures. I sure was hoping for the latter. "Have a good night. Stay warm."

I wasn't sure Liam heard my reply, but it didn't matter. He had probably already joined his friends and colleagues, leaving me to wonder just what was in store for Friday night. I held the phone against my scarf and jacket as I allowed myself a few minutes of privacy to daydream.

"Was that call about Strifle, dearie?" Mazie asked in earnest, suddenly materializing beside me as if she'd been my passenger all along. She delicately held the saucer and teacup in her hand as she waited for my reply. "All I heard was the tail end where you said *thanks for checking in*. Well? What's the progress? Did you find the guilty party yet? It was that gold-digger, wasn't it?"

It took me a few seconds to catch my breath. My rapid heart rate was another matter altogether.

"Mazie, you're getting as bad as Ted when it comes to sneaking up on me." Did being scared to the point of chest pain shave off years of one's life? "I saw on a movie once where the air gets really cold right before a spirit appears. I noticed the temperature changes during your visit much later. Think we could switch that around for my health?"

Mazie's light laughter was as delicate as the china in her hands. She didn't seem too bothered by the fact that she could induce my death in the blink of an eye. My heart was getting a workout lately. It made sense, though, considering she wasn't disturbed in the least by the fact that she was dead.

"Catch me up on your little investigation," Mazie encouraged me, looking out the windshield as if we were going on a trip. "Do you have any inkling where Strife could be?"

"I've managed to dig up a name who can help me with figuring out the identities of those witches and warlocks on the council," I offered up, wincing upon how flimsy that sounded. "He's a possible contact with the coven, although he doesn't seem to have a phone number where I can reach him. I was contemplating a drive up to Windsor, but I've been told that might not be such a good idea. You know, showing up uninvited and all."

Now that I had Mazie by my side to ask questions without Leo chiming in every two seconds, this could be my chance to find out more information that could solve this little mystery in short order so that I might enjoy my date with Liam on Friday night.

"Who might that be, my dear?"

"Merrick Bronach." Would Mazie recognize the name? I watched her expression closely. It was quite odd to see her frown, yet also see the silhouette of the trees outside the passenger side window. "I take it that you know him?"

"Yes, I do." Mazie's essence began to ebb in and out, indicating that she was losing the energy needed to stay on this side of the veil. "Merrick isn't who you..."

And just like that, Mazie gradually evaporated into thin... cold...air.

Finally! You'd think that woman had nothing better to do.

A tiny scream erupted from my throat as Leo popped into the passenger seat that Mazie had just vacated.

"Are you, Ted, and Mazie in cahoots to give me a one-way ticket to the other side?" I exclaimed, unable to keep my irritation at bay any longer. Unlike Mazie, there was nothing preventing me from putting a bell on his collar and fastening it around Leo's neck. "Stop doing that or I'll put that bell on you!"

I found the spell that will allow you to speak with Merrick Bronach without physically putting us all at death's door. You just need to cast it very carefully, if you know what I mean.

"You're exaggerating about death's door, Leo." Technically, I wasn't so sure that was the case given what Mazie was trying to tell me right before she disappeared, but I'm sure death wouldn't be the end result. A toad, maybe. But death? No. Of that, I was certain. "But I agree that we should probably try to contact Mr. Bronach through other channels."

Will wonders never cease? You're open to other opinions besides your own.

I quickly turned the engine off and gathered my things, wanting to be inside where hopefully Ted had started a fire in the hearth. The rush of cold air coming in off the shoreline had me losing my breath briefly as I got out of the car. I made it through the front gate that practically groaned when I opened it and was at the front door at the precise moment Ted swung it open from the inside to reveal...

Well, I didn't expect that.

Unfortunately, my fight or flight instinct didn't kick in the way I'd come to rely on over these past few months. The energy that usually gathered in the palm of my hand had failed me to the nth degree. My favorite pair of black knee-high boots seemed to be frozen in place, which technically wasn't out of the question seeing as how cold it was this evening.

In case you didn't realize it, we might be in trouble.

"Ms. Marigold, I presume?"

An older gentleman was standing beside Ted as if the two of them were best buddies. Ted was even attempting to give me that endearing smile that had melted my heart upon first sight, showing a bit of his chipped teeth. As for his newfound friend, the elderly man was rather distinguished looking and his kind expression had me somewhat confused as to his purpose.

Honestly, I wasn't sure what to think about this bizarre encounter.

What was this stranger doing in my house?

Pssst.

"Yes, I'm Raven Marigold," I replied, following an innate need to answer the man. What I really wanted to do was demand to know why he was in my home. Upon further reflection, why had Ted allowed such thing to happen? "You're Merrick Bronach."

You had to state the obvious? I'm sure he's impressed beyond words.

I wasn't sure how I was aware of this man's identity, but I knew it all the same. I also realized that my composed response wasn't natural. I should literally be screaming for help, running toward my car, or dialing 911.

You're just now figuring that out? Witchcraft, Raven, witchcraft. Merrick is using some sort of spell, and you're going to have to break it if we stand a chance of—

Whatever Leo had been going to say was cut off, and with very good reason. Had I been my normal self, I might have recognized just how out of hand this current situation of ours had become.

Duck!

Duck?

Goose!

Leo's directive didn't make sense to me at the time. Instead, I could only stand by and look on in disbelief as two apparitions began to gradually form on either side of me. Neither Mazie nor Lucille looked happy with the man currently standing beside Ted.

Before Mr. Bronach, Ted, or myself could utter a word, a battle of wills originated on my doorstep with a brilliant flash. The force of energy coming from Mazie and Lucille had me stumbling backward and eventually landing in a small snowdrift with a plop. By the time my eyesight adjusted, Ted stood alone in the doorway looking a little worse for wear with his blondish white hair standing on end and what appeared to be soot on his chin.

I told you to duck, you silly goose.

Nine

~~~

"I've witnessed my first battle between beings existing on the ethereal versus astral planes of existence...and lived to tell the tale," I exclaimed in utter disbelief, lifting my wine glass in salute to no one in particular. It didn't matter that my fingers were still trembling at the thought of having been on the receiving end of a charm spell that had suppressed my true natural reaction to the situation. The fact that I'd perceived such a sight without reacting in my own defense had me a bit rattled and jacked up on adrenaline. "Goose, Leo? Really?"

I panicked. It tends to happen when I'm magically ambushed by someone using an astral projection spell in combination with various other offensive invocations.

Ted and I were sitting in the living room in front of the fireplace while Leo was stretched out on the coffee table cleaning his right paw as if nothing was amiss. As for Mazie and Lucille, they'd vanished right along with Merrick Bronach.

None of us were certain what happened to the two apparitions as a result of their various forms of attack and their innate exposure inherent to each plane's differing set of physics. I could only assume the discharge of such energies had depleted their resources to stay on this side of the veil. They were probably cast back to their proper individual point of travel.

"We should call your mother, Miss Raven."

Leo's left eye twitched.

"No," I immediately replied to Ted, who clearly didn't understand the ramifications of his suggestion. A colossal amount of wine to settle my nerves was the proper prescription for my expert diagnosis. "Absolutely not. A thirty-year-old woman cannot continue to rely on her mother every time she is attacked by magical beings traveling on other planes to attack me for looking into other people's business. Besides, that's what Leo is for. Handling the day-to-day business of magical combat."

Although, there was helping and then there was *helping*.

"Goose? Really?"

Could we please stop rehashing my faux pas and focus on our options moving forward?

"And what options would those be, Leo?" I tilted my head back against the cushion and closed my eyes. This supernatural stuff wasn't getting any easier the way I'd hoped. Neither was attempting to even out my breathing, but that didn't stop me from continuing to try. "Merrick Bronach clearly has the upper hand and experience. I thought he was a friendly older warlock who had helped my mother at some point in her life, but I'm beginning to think otherwise now. He clearly didn't want me to find him. From the multipronged offense strategy he'd unleashed during his unexpected visit—which I'm pretty sure was in self-defense—and the fact that he could control my native responses, surely it's a notable sign that he's a very powerful warlock."

I hate to say this, but...

"Then don't say it," I warned Leo, bringing my head forward a little too fast. I blinked away the double vision to focus on only one orange and black cat instead of the initial two I had in my vision. Dual Leos would have definitely sent me straight to a mental institution...do not pass go. "We're *not* calling my mother. Absolutely not, though something does have me curious. How did Merrick Bronach even know that I was trying to reach him? Could it be possible he was here to answer our inquiries?"

"That is highly doubtful," Ted answered while lifting his large hand and attempting to smooth down his blondish white hair that was still somewhat untidy from the blow he suffered from the blast of energy that had smacked into him.

You said yourself that Merrick was a talented warlock who wasn't to be trifled with. Can we just go along with that assumption and slam the lid on this case?

"Mazie and Lucille slammed something into Mr. Bronach, and it wasn't a lid from what I could tell." I tapped my finger on the side of the wine glass as I ran through our options. "It's too dangerous to use that spell you advised earlier, Leo, isn't it? I mean, Mr. Bronach would most likely be waiting for me to contact him through magic. After the attack Mazie and Lucille unleashed, it's not unwise to believe that he might retaliate. Who knows what that wizard would do once he had me trapped? Then again, Mazie and Lucille might have blasted him into another plane of existence. I don't know much about science, but I'm pretty sure the negative material plane would destroy him on contact."

Are you going to tell Mazie the bad news, or am I? This little game has become far too dangerous to prolong any further.

"Leo, it's not that simple." I wasn't going to be able to get on board with Leo's train of thought with Strifle still missing.

"You said yourself that Strifle was probably in a good deal of pain being forcibly separated from Mazie. How can we just stand back and pretend nothing is wrong while someone suffers?"

"Miss Raven has a point, Leo."

You tell that oversized lump of wax that I didn't ask for his opinion. He could very easily end up as a bunch of candles if we run into that warlock again.

"No." I wasn't going to hurt Ted's feelings just because Leo was a scaredy cat and acting out. "I'm going to finish this glass of wine, we're going to find a spell that can protect me while I'm astrosurfing or whatever it's called, and we're going to get the answers we need."

Those words came out surprisingly confident considering that I was probably more afraid than Leo was at the moment. I'm not ashamed to admit that I downed the glass of red wine to gain the fortitude I'd need for this almost impossible incantation.

You're going to die there while we watch from here. You cannot leave me here with Ted—the candlemaker. Or worse, your mother—the wicked witch.

"What does happen to you if..." Saying the D word was like jinxing myself, so I reworded my question. "What happens when I'm old and grey, getting ready to pass on? Do you come with me or are you no longer linked to anyone?"

Truthfully, the thought of crossing the veil without Leo by my side was unimaginable. It was easy now to see how selfless Nan had been in her bid to leave Leo behind to help guide me through my witchcraft journey, which more than demonstrated her love for me.

And she wouldn't want you to die before your journey even

had a chance to begin. There. Decision made. We can now tell Mazie we're not continuing with the case.

"No, Leo." If anything, knowing the lengths Nan had gone to in order for me to have Leo by my side only fortified my decision to find Strifle. I peered into my empty glass, but then thought better of having more wine. "Let's do this for Mazie and Strifle."

Or not. Is there something you're losing in translation here? I thought I was rather clear in my opinion.

Leo rolled over onto his back and stayed in that spot the entire time I browsed through the grimoire looking for something I could use. The various invocations inside the section on protection spells were rather unsettling, but I persevered until I finally found an incantation that could help us.

"Leo?" A quick look at the clock told me that it was after ten o'clock at night. Ted had absconded a while ago, but he'd left several ingredients in his wake that could potentially come in handy. I just hoped that whichever ones were needed weren't something so unique that it was impossible to get in the spur of the moment. "What do you think of this one?"

Does it protect you against a warlock casting a spell on you?

"Yes."

I'd read over that part twice to make sure.

Will it work while you're astroplaning?

"Yes," I replied, having already considered that tiny issue.

I was quite proud of myself.

How long does the invocation last?

"Long enough for me to ask the questions I need and then get back to my body."

Answering the question like that had me a little excited that I was about to attempt my first astroplaning trip. If this worked, maybe I could visit Heidi or my mother in New York.

What about the house?

"The house?"

Yes, our house...the one I'll currently be in while you jet off to some other place.

Okay, I was a bit lost by that inquiry. Then again, this was one of the main reasons that Leo had been left behind with me. I couldn't get upset with him triple checking everything when that was part of his job description.

"What does the house have anything to do with me casting a...ohhhh."

Now Leo's question made sense. Merrick Bronach could easily cast a spell—an offensive conjuration known as arcane magic, in this case—on my surroundings, thereby affecting my body, and thus disturbing what I was trying to accomplish by simply burning me to ash. I read the spell for the eighth time, contemplating on whether or not the house was included in the sphere of the protection spell.

"Aha!" I replied in victory, very proud that I'd made it this far. "Yes, it does! It protects against offensive spells cast with an area of effect on one hundred yards from where I'm casting my own incantation."

, I bit my lower lip as I waited for Leo to come up with another question that might put a wet blanket over my excitement. He was still draped over the coffee table, but the audible sigh told me that he didn't have any other requirements of the evocation/abjuration spells I'd chosen.

One qualified as an evocation, because it harnessed the power of the elements for extraplanar travel. The other was an abjuration due to its ability to provide me protection while doing so. The safety zone extended to my physical body and that of my conscious mind while it projected.

What is it that we're doing again? I lost my train of thought.

It was never a good sign when Leo forgot where we were in the conversation. He ever so slowly stood on all four paws before plopping down on his haunches to clean the same paw he'd been nursing when I walked through the door as if the last four and a half hours hadn't occurred at all.

I don't want you to think that I haven't attempted to fix this little memory problem of his, but apparently there was some unwritten rule where a witch couldn't undo the consequences left behind by dark magic. It was almost akin to sewing up a tear in the fabric of reality. One could stitch them up, but the edges were still there no matter how tight you pulled them together.

On the other hand, there were bonuses to Leo's condition.

"We're going to cast a spell so that I can speak with Merrick Bronach." I quickly shifted the grimoire so that it was tilted against one of the pestles, all but moving Leo out of my way. It wasn't such a bad thing that he couldn't remember what all took place from the time we'd arrived home. He'd talk me through the process without any criticism or his witty remarks. "I'll quickly cast a powerful protection spell before attempting the evocation that enables the astroprojection."

There was no time to waste with Leo's memory issue. Should it return full force, I wasn't so sure he'd still be giving his full support in casting these particular spells. Within minutes, everything was set up for me to begin my journey.

You're in an awful big hurry. Is there something I should know?

"There's always things you should know, Leo." It was best I not lie or he would see right through me. "Right now, I'm hoping you'll guide me through the rest of this protection spell."

A bit of protection is always good, I guess.

Guilt flooded my system, but I didn't let that stop me from getting comfortable on the oversized burgundy pillow that I used as a cushion when casting spells. Leo followed my lead and settled down as if he were getting ready to watch squirrels chase one another in the front lawn.

Wait a second. Is there a reason we're doing this specific protection spell?

If I mentioned fairies, there was no doubt that Leo's memory would return with a bang. It probably wasn't wise to bring up Mazie or Lucille's previous visit, either.

That meant not answering Leo and concentrating on the page in the grimoire that would offer me a bit of safety before paying Mr. Bronach a surprise visit in return for his abrupt earlier one.

Generating an abjuration in combination with an evocation of such proportions meant drawing as much energy from the earth as I could muster. I was beginning to do so a lot easier than I had in the beginning, though don't get me wrong—I was as accident prone with casting these different types of magic as I was walking on two legs. That was the very reason I concentrated on the words in front of me as if my life depended on it—because it did.

Did you mention fairies?

Uh-oh.

Leo could read my thoughts as easily as he could understand my words. I should have attempted to block my mental deliberations, but it was too late. Just as it was too late for Leo to prevent me from completing the abjuration.

I'd already begun the spell and could literally sense the energy absorbing into my body with each verse of the incantation.

Guardians of the night

Protect me with all your might
Far, wide, and with great height
Cast your protection about me tight
And of all within sight

The warmth that invaded my being had nothing to do with the blazing fire behind me. The ardent elemental power from within the earth continued to flow into me as I bound each material component carefully into the offering. When all the correct roots, herbs, and flower petals were added, I then used the mortar to carefully grind the components together while never hesitating over the words in front of me.

Imagine the zone of protection, oh deceitful one. Cast it wide. Make it impenetrable.

A part of me realized that Leo had finally discovered the reason we needed the protection spell, but he was wise enough to follow through in his responsibility to be my guide without disrupting and thus destroying the magic.

"That was exhilarating!" I whispered, quickly finding the delicate page that contained the astroplane invocation. "We need to keep going, Leo."

You can die happy then. Do you realize the danger that you're putting us in by...

It was crucial that I didn't lose the energy coursing through my veins, nor give Leo the chance to prevent me from seeing this through to the end. His lecture gradually faded away as I began to recite the evocation that would have my conscious mind leaving my body behind.

I should have been terrified of the prospect, or at least tentative. This was a rather giant step in my witchcraft education, and there was something inside of me that couldn't allow Strife to be in pain any longer than necessary.

Body and spirit

Together but separate
Not one but two
Will always remain true

There were more verses, which I continued to read aloud without hesitation, maintaining my rhythm and timing. I stayed the course, but I wasn't truly prepared for what came next. One minute I was focusing on the delicate page in the grimoire...and then I wasn't.

What do you see, Raven?

Leo sounded so far away, yet I could feel his presence beside me. It was rather surreal, and I suddenly found myself rising up in the middle of a dark forest. There had been no hesitation, no tunnel that I'd traveled through to get here...my presence had just shifted to another place in a second of time. I was buffeted by gentle winds on either side of me, as if adrift in a warm place separate from the scene before me.

What was even more strange was that I could sense that it was cold around me, but I somehow remained warm as I began to walk through the bare winter trees searching for...

I don't know why I was brought here instead of to the location of Merrick Bronach.

You were drawn to that place for a reason, Raven. Concentrate. Look around for what has enticed you there, and then put yourself back into your physical body pronto.

I'd never thought in a million years that I would hear something like that, but the supernatural existence of things had altered my reality.

Stop walking, Raven. See everything around you, inhale the scents, and listen closely for perceptible sounds to draw you closer to your target. That's right. Use your senses to guide you through this maze.

I did as Leo suggested, though the area around me was

rather stark and terrifying in appearance. There were no beautiful songbirds singing to one another, there was nothing in sight with the exception of ancient trees without their leaves, and the shadows continued to darken as if they wanted to swallow me whole. It was as if I was the only individual in existence here in the woods.

Focus, Raven.

Leo was my physical tether to reality, and I didn't want to lose his guidance. As a matter of fact, I was seriously contemplating abandoning this spell to return back home. The excitement of trying something unimaginable had worn off completely as the stark reality of this dark forest had set in. In its place was a growing terror that I wouldn't be able to find my way back home to the warmth of my own place and time.

Listen...

Leo's encouragement to do one more thing had me picking up the faintest murmur of voices. I slowly began to advance in that direction, surprised when my steps didn't make a sound on the damp leaves underneath me. It seemed I was able to use some of my senses while others were ineffectual and materially bound to my physical body.

I blinked several times at the sight of a small cottage tucked away in...

Wait.

I couldn't believe what I was seeing, but there was no denying the charming neighborhood that appeared before me. Lights shone bright from their windows, smoke rose from their chimneys, and the golden rays from the streetlamps glistened off the winding roads between each row of numerous properties.

Pay attention, Raven! You must concentrate.

Could Leo literally perceive what I was seeing? Or did he

know me well enough by now that my silence meant I'd deterred from the task at hand? Either way, his directive had me focusing on the quaint backyard of a specific house where a woman was being ushered inside by...

Oh.

Oh, what? What does oh *mean? Raven? What do you see?*

Apparently, Leo couldn't perceive what my gaze had landed on...better yet, who.

Merrick Bronach.

I froze in my tracks when the powerful warlock remained standing in the doorway after permitting a woman to enter his home, even going so far as to gesture with his hand that I should follow.

Ten

"We've been waiting for your arrival."

Wow. Talk about an ominous statement. Warlock Bronach isn't very friendly, is he?

I'm not exactly sure how I did it, but one minute I was at the edge of a wooded tree line, and then the next I was standing in the middle of a living room with a raging fire burning in the hearth. Apparently, the *we* Merrick Bronach had been referring to were the three other women in attendance.

It was then I put two and two together and came up with... the council.

Be very careful, Raven. Return to your body the second you get a hint of danger. There is no need to overextend yourself.

I didn't respond to either Leo or Mr. Bronach's declaration. Instead, I took the time to study my surroundings. The small house resembled a typical New England cottage, though I could see stairs on the far side of the wall leading up to a second level. The home was designed in rich dark wood from floor to ceiling. It wasn't surprising to find that earth tones dominated the décor. This home was obviously owned by a man.

Two of the women were guests in Mr. Bronach's home while one resided here, not that I could figure out how I was certain of that small detail. I could only assume that the two seated on the couch were the guests and the one standing by the fire slept underneath this roof each and every night. The witch over by the hearth seemed to have an instant dislike for me, though I couldn't imagine why. I'd never met her before in my life. I was not in competition with her for anything.

What does she look like? Maybe I know her.

Those gathered here matched the very description that Mazie had given those on the council. I'd apparently interrupted a council meeting, and everyone in this room was a suspect.

Isn't that handy?

"You sought *me* out, Mr. Bronach," I replied tentatively, ignoring Leo's rhetoric and trying not to give away what I'd figured out about their positions here in the coven. I'd wanted to remind this warlock that he'd been in my house uninvited. Come to think of it, his unexpected visit had been quite rude. I decided it was safer for me to remain where I stood just inside the doorway while I pointed that little tidbit out. "Mazie Rose Young felt as if she was protecting me against you. It seems as if her familiar didn't cross over to the other side with her, and she asked me to find out why."

Why is it that you give so much information away in the first meeting? It's like you just have to dip your fingers in red paint to draw a bullseye on your forehead.

I figured if Merrick Bronach knew I was looking for him to begin with, I wasn't telling him anything he didn't already know. It was really quite simple. Mazie wanted Strifle returned to her in the afterlife. I needed to figure out why her familiar was prevented from doing so in the first place before succeeding in the latter.

It didn't escape me that my mother had thought Merrick Bronach was trustworthy. Apparently, he'd done well for himself over the years. A councilmember? I couldn't imagine he could climb any higher in rank.

"Correct me if I'm wrong, but wasn't it you who was looking for a way to reach me, Miss Marigold?" Merrick Bronach joined the older woman standing by the fire. He stood on the opposite side of the mantel, but it was clear they were putting on a united front. He was rather on the thin side, but that didn't stop him from crossing his arms in intimidation. "I was simply attempting to make your quest easier."

"A simple phone call would have sufficed. Instead, you broke into my home." How had Mr. Bronach known I'd been given his name in the first place? Was the council really that powerful? Did he have some warlock antennae that alerted him to whenever someone mentioned his name? There was a nursery rhyme like that, and one that technically should have terrorized me as a child now that I understood its true meaning. "I can see you have guests, and I don't want to keep you. I simply wanted to know...why?"

"She looks just like Rosemary at that age, doesn't she?" one of the women on the couch murmured as she held a delicate cup to the side. Did every witch drink tea? Maybe I was defective, but I'd have to worry about that later. "Same high cheekbones, same defined jawline, and those green eyes...my oh my. One and the same."

Is that Hestia? I'd recognize that voice anywhere. That means Ruby isn't far away. Stay away from those two, Raven. They're worse than fairies, and that's saying something.

"I was thinking the same thing, Hestia." The redheaded

middle-aged woman had proven Leo right, and she must be Ruby. "It's not just her looks, you know. She's following in her grandmother's heretical footsteps. What a disgrace. At least Rosemary's daughter had the common sense to give up practicing altogether rather than blaspheme the faith. Can you imagine what the other covens think of us, allowing such a heresy to exist?"

Why that...Ruby's a mean witch!

It was easy to see why Mazie thought this council was responsible for Strifle's abduction. They all seemed a little too hoity-toity, if you know what I mean. All I had to do now was narrow it down, declare the reason I was here, and look for any signs of guilt across their well-preserved faces.

"You two do realize that I can hear you, right?" I asked, wondering if this spell I'd cast only allowed Merrick Bronach that privilege. I was beginning to feel the physical effects of the spell separating my conscious self from my body, and I probably didn't have long before the invocation wore off. It was best I inquire about Strifle and leave immediately, before something happened that I couldn't control. "I will have you know that my grandmother was able to help many people after she left this coven, and my mother has no regrets in distancing herself from the likes of you."

I didn't mean for you to instigate the coven, Raven. I was only expressing my view, which you seem to have taken as incentive to antagonize the very council whom could make our lives rather difficult if they so desired. Give an inch, you take a gosh darn mile. I really should know that about you by now.

The collective gasps that traveled around the room told me I might have overstepped my bounds, but these witches didn't get to criticize my family while I was kept on some invisible leash. That right was reserved only for me. They needed to keep quiet.

And me. I quite enjoy being critical of your mother's choices from time to time. Who am I kidding? I love getting under that woman's skin on a regular basis.

"We have no idea why Strife didn't follow Mazie into the afterlife, Miss Marigold." Instead of Merrick Bronach being the one to answer, it was the woman standing next to the fireplace. She was tapping her long red fingernails on the wooden mantel as she studied me a little too vigilantly, almost as if she were looking for a weakness to exploit. She had to be in her mid-sixties, but I don't believe she had any intention of giving up what youth she could sustain. "Don't think it escaped Merrick's notice that the familiar residing in your house was none other than Rosemary's familiar. Nor did he miss the creature your grandmother thought to create without regard to how her careless actions might affect the reputation of this coven. Merrick is being too kind in letting those atrocities go without punishment. You may leave now and never come back."

"Now, now," Mr. Bronach chided, raising a hand to scratch his rather square chin. "That's no way to treat our guest, Angelica."

Angelica must be the gold-digger, not that I was name-calling. I was just repeating what Mazie thought of the woman standing next to the powerful warlock who must be the council leader. Saying she was dressed to the nines was an understatement.

Ugh. I forgot about her. What is that creature even doing there? That woman has undermined or ambushed almost every witch in the coven. She's not well-liked, you know. On a side note, take the pass that old warlock has given us and vamoose back home.

"It's true, Merrick. This was supposed to be our honeymoon, and yet we're here dealing with—this hedge-witch gone rogue."

"Did Mazie happen to say what it's like on the other side?" Hestia asked with a somewhat trusting gaze, cutting off whatever Angelica had been going to say. Hestia was the most likeable out of these four individuals, but that wasn't saying much. "I had a vision recently, you know."

Oh, that's never good. Poor thing. Going back to this honeymoon announcement, I'm shocked. Talk about scandalous!

I was too focused on Hestia's vision to worry about who was married to who. You see, there are some witches who are intuitive enough to *see* their own death. I'm not sure he or she actually saw the reason, so much as they were aware his or her death was increasingly imminent. Apparently, Nan had seen her death—it was the sole reason that she was able to cast a spell for Leo to remain behind while she crossed the veil.

Speaking of a veil, I'm still in shock that Merrick would have chosen Angelica over Vivian. Oh, to have been a fly on the wall. I'd say he was a cradle robber, but does age really matter once you reach your seventies for the second or third time?

"Hestia, could you imagine leaving your familiar here...in pain...while your soul went to the afterlife?" I figured she would the easiest witch to obtain information from considering her situation. "I've heard it's very painful for them. What is your familiar? A cat? A fairy?"

You just had to ask, didn't you?

"Oh, no," Hestia said with a laugh, ignoring everyone's glares aimed in her direction. I'd definitely made the right decision in targeting her for answers. "My familiar is a cockroach.

He's around here somewhere. Always expanding his clan in one place or another."

I wasn't particularly fond of cockroaches, so I began looking around for anything remotely resembling such a filthy insect. Depending on where one lived in New York City, those little buggers were everywhere.

Harold won't appreciate you calling him a filthy insect. Surprisingly, he keeps himself conspicuously clean.

"Hestia, we've talked about you bringing Harold into this house," Angelica chastised with a frown. She, too, began searching the hardwood floor for any sign of the six-legged creature. "Merrick, do something to rid us of these pests."

"We still have an important guest in our home," Merrick warned, bringing everyone's attention back to the reason of my visit. They all made it seem as if someone astroplaning across the prime material plane was the most natural thing in the world. The coven must use witchcraft on a daily basis. "Miss Marigold, we know nothing about Strifle and why she didn't follow Mazie into the afterlife."

The council knows nothing. There. You have your answer, Raven. Now let's wrap things up. You're becoming quite pale here, you know.

I didn't doubt I was losing a bit of color. It was becoming harder and harder to keep myself separate from my physical being. My only problem was that I didn't believe Merrick Bronach for one second.

The only thing I could not figure out was if the entire council was in on Strifle's abduction or only one of the members was responsible for such a crime.

Don't make this an issue. Warlock Bronach said he didn't know anything, and that's that. We can now tell Mazie we tried, move Heidi to Paramour Bay, and live happily ever after.

"Mr. Bronach, I've been hired to find out what has happened to Strifle and see to it that she is safely delivered to Mazie on the other side," I declared over Leo's long drawn-out moan, which resounded a little bit too loudly in my head. He was really not happy with my decision to push the issue. "I have one question for you. Is it normal for the four of you to meet on a Tuesday evening or did it take the lot of you to force your way into my home?"

The way Hestia's pink lips formed a perfect O gave me an answer. Ruby muttered something about the Marigolds not always minding their own business, and Angelica's red nails were now curled into the palms of her hands. I had to remind myself that these witches couldn't hurt me in this form, and that I'd also cast a protection spell around the house.

Raven, where's Ted?

"The four of you must have come together this evening to talk about me, and the fact that Mazie wants to find her familiar," I summarized, taking a guess and hoping it paid off. Hestia's O got a little bigger, and Ruby practically knocked the woman's tea out of her hands with a thwack on the arm. The way Merrick Bronach's' lips were thinning even more so than usual told me that I was on to something. "There's only one choice here."

Oh, no. No, no, no, no, no. There are a lot of choices here, Raven. A ton, if you must know. It is not nice to give them an ultimatum. Did you not just hear what I said? I haven't seen Ted for quite some time. We really should check on his whereabouts before you go and get us into something Ted can't get out of, if you know what I mean.

"Miss Marigold, I would think very carefully before you go any further down that road," Merrick Bronach cautioned, taking a step forward. His weathered features made it easy to assume he was offering kind advice, though I highly doubted he had good intentions. "The four of us did come together this evening to talk about Mazie's situation, but it wasn't for the reason you have surmised. We had nothing to do with Strifle's abduction."

"I never said that Strifle had been abducted." I slowly smiled, not usually gaining the upper hand so easily. This was quite fun, especially since my physical being was far away from this place of danger. The satisfying feeling was quite a power jolt. "I only said that Strifle didn't follow Mazie into the afterlife."

You're going to get more than a jolt if you don't stop running your mouth.

"What Merrick is trying to say is that if Strifle didn't go with Mazie, we can only assume the little pixie was abducted or simply didn't wish to follow. We already have a number of enemies, Raven, though you wouldn't know that seeing as you aren't a part of the coven." Angelica stepped forward, shifting so that it appeared she joined her husband in unison. Upon further thought, this woman wasn't to be trifled with, but I'd already jumped in with both feet. "We are here this evening to put our heads together in hopes of coming up with an answer, but it seems we have no information that could help you in your quest. Might I suggest you speak with some of the witches and warlocks in Stamford. There has always been a bit of bad blood between our two covens, especially where Mazie was concerned."

Of course, Angelica isn't to be trifled with. Does she still have those red nails that look like daggers? Those things could rip out an eye. I wonder if Vivian now wears a patch?

"I find it hard to believe you would have already heard

what Ruby had to say this evening considering she basically arrived the same time I did," I pointed out, wondering where my bravery was coming from.

Maybe because you're not really there? Think of astroplaning like social media—you can hide behind a computer while saying the most outrageous things without any repercussions.

"As we've said, we have no information that could help you in your quest," Mr. Bronach stated as if this conversation had drawn to a close. He even rested a hand on Angelica's lower back, as if being near her gave him confidence. Hmmm. Maybe that was the reason he'd chosen Angelica over Vivian. "Should that change, I'll reach out to you...by phone, this time around. I wouldn't want to upset Mazie or her friend into another tizzy."

That's right. I had Mazie and Lucille on my side, and they were way better than any computer. There wasn't much time left, so I'd better make my position known.

You don't have to do that, you know. There's such a thing as "leaving in peace". You should try it. It sets the tone so well.

"One of you, if not all, knows exactly what happened to Strifle." I was almost yanked away from Windsor as the spell finally wore off, but I managed to hold on for ten more seconds. It was quite a feat, and I was rather proud of my effort. "You have exactly twenty-four hours to return Strifle to me before I come here in person...and I won't be alone."

It should be noted that astroplaning back into one's body was similar to the sensation of being sucked into the engine of a jet. The struggle was real. When I finally slammed back into my physical shell, my arms were still flailing from grasping at the edges of my reality. How I didn't fall back into my fireplace was a miracle.

And just what army do you think you're going to scrounge up to go marching into Windsor? I want it on record that I don't look good in camouflage utilities.

Eleven

"You did what?"

I have a feeling you didn't read that question with enough emphasis. I was on the phone with my mother attempting to explain what had taken place last night. Unfortunately, I haven't been able to explain anything successfully past the astroplane evocation. Honestly, maybe it was better she didn't know that I'd basically declared war on the Windsor coven if Strife wasn't returned this evening by midnight.

Among other things that Mom didn't know was the fact that the power I was drawing from my environment was becoming easier, and my strength was reaching new levels. I couldn't help but think that the occasional hints that Leo and my mother had been dropping in relation to the timing of my birth and my lineage might have something to do with some powerful alignment.

It sounded odd, but I was beginning to visualize how the power of the earth could be funneled toward a certain objective using my ability acting as a conduit...or maybe my newfound power had gone to my head.

What *had* I been thinking to issue an ultimatum to the council?

You weren't thinking. That is *the problem. You basically used a flamethrower to light a pipe.*

Other than a few wisecracks here and there, Leo hadn't been talking to me.

"Mom, I'll call you back," I said with a little too much relief once I saw someone making their way across the street from the diner. I couldn't make out who it was or if he or she was even stopping into the store, but the excuse gave me a reprieve. "I have customers headed my way."

I hung up before Mom was able to say anything to freak me out any more than I already was, considering I was on pins and needles waiting for something dire to pop up. It would probably be best to do another longer-lasting protection spell.

You're just lucky we were able to find Ted. We could have easily stumbled upon a puddle of melted wax instead of Mazie and Lucille holding him for safekeeping.

"How was I to know that Ted would be outside the radius I'd put into place?" I grumbled, wondering if there would ever come a time I could cast a spell without having to listen to the list of ramifications from Leo or my mother for hours on end. "What was Ted doing in town that late at night? Don't answer that. He was probably visiting that mannequin he fancies."

Ted's infatuation with the mannequin in Mindy's boutique was bordering on obsession, but what was the harm in falling in love with an inanimate object? Don't think I haven't considered giving the mannequin a life of her own, especially if Ted were to ask for such a favor.

Ted's love life is the least of our worries. What would possess you to give the Windsor coven an ultimatum when they might not be the culprits? Oy vey, there's not enough premium catnip in existence to lower my current stress level.

"Leo, is that—"

The bell above the glass door chimed before I could finish asking my question.

He's here about Heidi! Raven, so help all things supernatural if you mess this one up...

Leo was referring to the fact that Beetle, the man who ran his own financial firm over on Oceanview Drive and was about ready to retire, had just walked through the door as if a tornado carried him inside with a gust of wind. He literally looked like a mad scientist with his white hair standing on end and his blue eyes bulging slightly from their sockets.

If you say those dreadful things remind you of me, I won't be responsible for my actions.

The only good thing to come of this was the fact that Leo was talking to me more than he had earlier this morning. With that said, I was quite baffled as to why Beetle would be stopping into the tea shop when he hadn't done so since my arrival in Paramour Bay.

"Good morning," I said with a smile, walking around the counter in hopes that he was here to buy something. Sales hadn't quite picked up since the holiday rush, and it would be nice to have new customers to start off the new year. "How can I help you today?"

"You look just like her," Beetle exclaimed in awe, reaching into the pocket of his rather worn dress coat to pull out a pair of round spectacles I didn't even know were still made in that style. He fumbled a bit to open the sides before setting them low on the bridge of his nose. "Well, I'll be. Just look at you! Look at you! Yes, yes. This will work out just fine."

I was a bit bewildered, not entirely understanding his statement.

You're not the only bewildered one. The man has always been a bit out there, if you know what I mean.

"I hope this works out, too, and that we find the right tea blend for your tastes." I was rather proud of myself for having steered the conversation away from Nan and toward a desired purchase. "It's nice to officially meet you. I'm Raven Marigold."

"Oh, I know, I know." It was the third time he'd repeated words or phrases. It was a cute idiosyncrasy. He almost dropped his briefcase when he exchanged hands in order to extend his right arm. "It's a pleasure to finally meet you, too. Oh! I almost forgot."

Beetle turned around in haste and walked back to the front door. For just a brief moment, I thought he was going to leave. Instead, he took down the help wanted sign that I'd taped to the glass entrance.

What. Is. He. Doing?

Leo usually had a habit of overreacting. This time? It was like a brick settled in my stomach, but I continued to smile as I talked myself into believing Beetle had taken down the sign due to wanting to refer someone for the job—you know, maybe a granddaughter or grandson.

I'm going insane. There's no other explanation.

"There's no need to look any further, my dear Raven," Beetle exclaimed with an excited glint to his blue eyes. He all but shoved the piece of paper toward me that I'd painstakingly spent an hour making. "I am closing the doors to my firm. At the same time, I'm looking for a way to keep busy. You know, I heard that the percentage rate of death after retirement is astronomical! Not me, though. Not me."

I honestly didn't think this day could get worse.

"Really?" I asked, giving myself time to think through this predicament I'd found myself in. I had enough on my plate with the Windsor coven. The more I thought about it, I think I might have gotten myself into more trouble than I could handle...hence the phone call to my mother. Maybe she'd be ready to hear the rest of my plight by the time I called her back. "Um, why retire at all then?"

What. Are. You. Doing? You're going to make a wreck of this whole thing.

Leo was apparently worried that I was going to ruin Heidi's chance to move to Paramour Bay, but that wasn't the case at all. I had a plan and—

Like your last plan worked out so well. I mean, you all but declared war on one of the most powerful witch covens that has existed since 1613. What's next? Are you going to set fire to my whiskers?

—it could make Heidi's transition easier, should she choose to make it.

"I'm closing in on sixty years old." Beetle walked over to the cash register and rested an elbow on the counter as if he were settling in to tell me a long story. Had this been any other day when I didn't have an angry coven on my heels, I would have enjoyed having such a distraction. "Sixty years old, my dear Raven. I've stared at numbers my entire life. I'm ready for a change. The way I see it, I can spare you an hour or two a day to learn the ropes while I'm closing out my clients. It sure would be nice to hand the reins over to someone, and I'm sure the shop owners can find someone in New Haven."

There's a curse on us. That's the only reason why each day with you at the helm seems to get worse and worse. Once again, I might be forced to resort to calling in your mother for reinforcements. Oh, how that pains me so, but you seem to never learn.

"Beetle, please don't take this the wrong way," I said tentatively, wondering how to go about turning down his offer for part-time help without hurting his feelings. "I can only offer a couple of dollars over minimum wage for now, and I was thinking the part-time position might be better suited to a college student who would be happy with what I can pay."

"I'm not working during my retirement years for the money, my dear Raven. I have what I need and all the benefits from years of being self-employed." Beetle raised a white bushy eyebrow that matched his hair as he scanned the items in the shop. "I've always been more of a coffee person myself, but it's good to broaden one's horizon...especially at my age. Yes, yes. This is going to work out perfectly, you'll see!"

No, no. This is not *working out. Tell him, Raven. Tell him. Don't make me bite him!*

It seemed Beetle's way of talking was contagious. On the other hand, I could totally relate to Beetle on the coffee addiction. Regardless, he wasn't the person for the job.

"Beetle, I truly appreciate you coming in to talk to me about the position." I walked past him so that I was on the other side of the cash register. "I'll take your interest under advisement as I go through my selection process."

There were no other applicants at this time, but I'm sure someone else would stop in by the end of the week. Candy mentioned yesterday that one of the younger girls who comes into the salon frequently had mentioned looking for part-time work. I think the potential candidate might have been Dee's niece, but I wasn't sure.

I'm sure. Give Candy a call, ask for the girl's name, and make it happen. We cannot waste time given the current situa-

tion. Oh, and tell Candy you'll throw in some free tea with hair growth benefits. That should seal the deal.

"There's no need to do that," Beetle said, expressing enthusiasm even a lone cup of coffee wouldn't give me. He waved a hand in my direction and shot me an infectious smile that I tried my best to be immune to. "You've already found yourself a new employee, my dear Raven."

Beetle slapped the counter with a thwack, as if he was proud of himself for closing the books on this little arrangement. His eagerness to work here was rather compelling.

All right, Raven. You've pushed me far enough today. Enough is enough. I'll handle this myself. I'm going for his ankle.

Oh, that couldn't be good. I quickly scurried around the counter with every intention of stopping Leo from doing something horrible—like perform one of those video moves where a cat launched himself at someone's leg.

Fortunately, Beetle heard the strangled meow come from across the shop and turned in Leo's direction. My inherited familiar certainly didn't have the most melodic tone to his voice.

"What in tarnation is that?" Beetle bellowed, leaning back against the counter as if he'd just had a near death experience. "I've never seen anything quite so..."

Leo had been in midstride in his hunting progress when Beetle's exclamation echoed throughout the shop. The potential ending to this situation was not going to be pleasant, and Leo's stalking was going to turn into a full-on attack with expanded claws and open maw that could tear out Beetle's Achilles tendon with ease.

Leo's left lid began to bulge more than usual.

I did the only thing I could, hoping that it didn't result in me going to the hospital for stitches. Within seconds, I found myself in between the two and closing one eye as I waited for Leo's claws to become embedded in my calf.

"My dear Raven, you have a very big heart," Beetle whispered in praise, finally releasing his jacket to pat me on the shoulder. "Everyone needs a home, and that sweet furball should have all the catnip in the world after what he's probably gone through. Now, I'll stop in tomorrow for my first lesson before I have to get to my office. April sixteenth will be my official start date, if that's alright. Isn't this just grand? Just grand, I tell you."

And as simple as that, I had a new part-time employee.

Beetle took his leave, but not before walking past Leo and giving him two pats on the head. It was mighty obvious that Leo wasn't sure how to react to Beetle's offer of kindness. On one hand, I'm sure the catnip comment made him want to have Beetle starting later today, but the man's immediate reaction to Leo's appearance had definitely been a rough start.

"Leo?" I asked tentatively, stepping forward when he hadn't moved a muscle. I mean, not even his whiskers were twitching. Had just the mere thought of Beetle working here sent Leo into a catatonic state? "I'm sure we can figure out a way to fix this. We can—"

You'll do no such thing. Did you not hear the man? I'm entitled to all the catnip in the world. He's hired. Sure, there are more cons than pros in hiring Beetle for a couple of hours a day, but I think I can handle the tradeoff. With enough premium catnip in my pipe, I won't care who you hire.

Leo's self-indulgence was taking a front seat, but at least the situation hadn't ended with either Beetle or me needing first aid or a prosthetic limb.

I highly doubted Leo's concession would last. One hour with Beetle tomorrow would certainly change his mind, and most likely mine. That was if there *was* a tomorrow given my recent declaration of war.

"We'll figure the Beetle situation out tomorrow," I muttered, moving on to more important things. The more time that passed, the more I recognized the danger I'd put us in by issuing an ultimatum to a coven of powerful witches. "Right now, we have to figure out a way to keep from us from dying before midnight."

Not to rub your nose in it, but whose fault is that exactly?

Twelve

This is it. The Windsor coven has struck, and boy...is it a low blow from a sector I never would have guessed they'd come at us from. Is this the sight we've been cursed with for the rest of our lives? Gouge my eyes out now. Go ahead.

This *sight* Leo was referring to was my mother standing on my doorstep in her battle uniform—a form fitting black leather jacket that appeared to be lined in red fleece, black knee-high boots that made me think twice about ever wearing my favorite pair again, and matching black leather pants that I would never have been able to get over my thighs with a can of lard.

"Mom?" It took me a moment to formulate my question, so I stepped back to let her inside the warmth of the cottage. A flurry or two decided to join me, but they didn't last long once they hit the hardwood floor. "Did you leave your Harley at the train station? What do you think you're doing?"

I should have asked specifically why my mother had felt compelled to suddenly come to Paramour Bay, followed by why she was dressed like a biker who'd just robbed a high-end leather store. Instead, I rubbed my eyes with my fingers. Leo's suggestion of a curse began to make more sense than anything else going through my mind.

It was completely possible the council had driven me mad.

I tried blinking. It's useless. Regina is still there...looking like something out of Easy Rider. *By the way, I've read the original screenplay and found it very stimulating...freedom of the road and all that. Five stars. Hands down an American classic.*

"After the mess you've gotten yourself into, we're going to need to be proactive." My mother gestured toward my peacock-colored skirt and emerald green turtleneck before she began to take off her black leathered gloves one finger at a time. "Go change. We don't have all night, and the drive to Windsor will cost us an hour we don't have."

Windsor? Is there no end to this black void that has become my life?

"Leo, you're coming with us. Pack your pipe."

Over my dead—

My mother arched an eyebrow and directed her somewhat daring gaze Leo's way. I've never seen him back down from anyone, but he wisely didn't finish his vow of death before breaking a sweat speech. To cover up his capitulation, he began to clean his front right paw somewhat distractedly.

I wouldn't allow you to take Raven up there without me, anyway.

"Mom, we cannot go up against a full coven of witches. Not on their ground," I protested, recognizing just how much I'd gotten us in over our heads. I mean, my mother drove all the way from New York City to fix what I'd stirred up, even though she'd given up witchcraft when she was pregnant with me. This certainly wasn't one of my finer moments. "The council members aren't going to return Strifle without a fight, and there's not a thing I can do about it. I should be grateful they haven't turned me into a toad already. I'd say our prospects are about the same as a snowball's chance in Hades."

"Leo, what have you been putting into my daughter's head?" Regina chastised, slapping the leather gloves against her hand with a frown. "I'm pretty sure that's just a witch's tale passed down from generation to generation. Nobody is going to end up as a toad."

It's always better to be safe than sorry. One doesn't need to be a Boy Scout to figure that one out.

"Pretty sure?" I repeated, not willing to take any chances. "Look, maybe I should do another astroplane evocation to offer my sincere apologies and plead for mercy."

"Raven, the damage is done. Apologies aren't going to be offered to anyone. Look, we can argue about this on the way." Regina tapped her watch numerous times to make her point. "Go change into something more suitable for a nighttime mission in cold weather."

"Suitable for what? What is it that you're thinking we can do? Are we going to be inserted into that fortress by parachute?" I had almost been afraid to ask that question, but I'd already gotten us in a boiling pot of hot water without thinking or being prepared. "Are we going to go talk to the council? I'm still thinking a heartfelt apology would go a long way. We can say it was due to my inexperience as a novice. We can even add on that I didn't understand who they were or what they represented."

"Suitable for breaking and entering, and maybe some rough terrain," my mother answered rather vaguely, looking down at her dark clothing. "We're sneaking into the coven's temple to retrieve Strifle, casting a spell that will erase every trace of our presence, and returning here to Paramour Bay where Mazie can collect her familiar for its journey."

I told you calling your mother was a bad idea. She's been playing too much Battlefield 3.

"Mom, are you crazy?"

You really need to ask that question aloud after she explained her plan?

"I'm of perfect sound, mind, and body, thank you," Regina replied with dignity before waving her gloves at me. "You said on the phone that you believe the council members are the ones who took Strifle. There's only one place in that town with enough concentrated power to entrap a fairy, so that's where we look first. Now get a move on. I don't have all night to get there and search for this missing Tinkerbell lookalike."

Whatever it is you're thinking, Raven, we need to reconsider our options.

"What if Mom's right?" I asked Leo, seriously considering changing into a black pair of jeans and a dark winter coat before following her lead. "I mean, we could have Strifle returned to Mazie before midnight tonight."

Who, by the way, hasn't paid us a visit recently. Do you think that's a coincidence?

"Currently, there's been no curse placed upon this house," my mother interjected in her attempt to downplay Leo's concern. "You started a war, Raven. We need to end it before there is one."

I completely forgot how ruthless your mother can be. Maybe she's on to something here.

Leo was right. My mother had always been rather spiteful, and I hadn't been sure she'd come to help me out of this bothersome situation I'd found myself in. It did cross my mind that she was doing this for more personal reasons. Either way, she'd already made up her mind. She was going to go with or without me, and I didn't want to be responsible of the latter without making darn sure her six was covered.

Not even your mother is a match for the council, Raven. She's driving us off to our deaths. Not even my premium catnip can make this trip a winning proposition.

I didn't have a pair of leather pants, but I did own a pair of black jeans and matching turtleneck. I quickly made my way up to the bedroom loft, changed into clothes more suitable for the unbelievable task we were about to stumble into, and secured my hair on top of my head with a black hairband.

"Mom, should we bring any ingredients?" I called down, wondering what herbs and roots I had on hand. "I can ask Ted for anything I don't have."

"We won't need ingredients, Raven."

There's nothing in the supernatural realm that can save us from our own stupidity.

I didn't say anything as I came down the spiral staircase, believing that Mom would explain why we didn't need to take any components listed from the grimoire with us. Mom remained silent, but she was tapping the toe of her boot in an obvious sign of impatience by the time I'd rejoined her.

It's an annoying habit, isn't it?

"What do you mean we won't need ingredients?" What had I missed? Even the simplest magic missile spell required a bit of charcoal as a type of earthly material component. "Mom, you haven't practiced witchcraft in over thirty years. Well, besides one here and there that I'm sure you did when I was a child. And you totally faked the spell at the wax museum a couple of weeks ago."

Please don't go there. I can only handle so much before the stress puts me six feet under.

"Did I?" My mother's perfectly shaped eyebrow raised once

more, the small gesture causing my stomach to sink a bit lower. I didn't even have time to brace myself for her announcement, nor when she shoved my black dress coat into my chest along with what looked like a wool watch cap. "I spent twenty-three years under your grandmother's tutelage. I was casting spells at four years old, better than the way you are now, and doing so a lot more efficiently by the age of ten. Those are lessons that one doesn't forget easily, Raven. The more you practice the craft, the more energy you can draw from the earth. Components of the earth are used for two reasons—either by novices or by certain spells that are too complex for a hedge witch's innate power. You're a novice."

You just had to go there. Regina, could we shelf this discussion for another time?

"No, she can't," I responded with irritation, wondering when Leo had been going to clue me in on this little-known witchcraft fact. "Mom, what about all the herbal teas that Nan made for her customers?"

Can I call shotgun?

Leo wasn't *with us*, with us. He'd vanished before we left the house, but his presence was nonetheless there to offer his two cents. And there was no way I was giving up riding in the passenger seat since only the two front seats were heated. Leo's fur would just have to do its job in the back.

I'm being railroaded. The least you could do is let me ride in comfort. I did call dibs.

"The herbal remedies your grandmother crafted are different types of spells. They are what we refer to as hedge witchcraft or simple remedies which happens to contain a small amount of magic." My mom opened the front door, barely giving me time to grab my purse when she all but ushered me out of the house. The bitter cold slammed into me instantly, taking with it my breath. "Evocations harness the power of elements that involve health. They have most always been ingested since the dawn of mankind. That's not likely to change, although there have been instances where a witch can heal with the simplest of touches using enchantments cast on items or the laying on of hands. And before you ask, your grandmother didn't have that gift."

"So, you're saying that the Marigolds *do* have a gift, and not just hedge witchcraft."

This again? I'm not sure I can ride with the two of you. How about I just meet you there?

I was quite pleased with how this conversation was turning out, because my mother and I have argued since Nan's death about what witchcraft meant to our family. It hadn't taken me long to slip my hands through the arms of my heavy wool jacket as we continued to make our way down the pathway to the gate. It appeared we were taking her vehicle instead of mine, but that wasn't much of a surprise. She had a brand-new model with heated leather seats that she refused to part with once she'd experienced them.

"Healing is a specific type of gift," my mother corrected, opening the gate and wincing when a squeak rang out that most likely reached downtown. She stepped to the side to let me pass, not stopping her explanation of why she was right and I was wrong. "Being just an average witch is a curse."

"That makes no sense," I argued, only stopping when headlights turned off the main road out of town and down the gravel path to park behind my mother's vehicle. Who could be visiting me this evening? "Uh-oh."

The vehicle turned out to be a black F150, and one I'd personally ridden in.

Sheriff Liam Drake.

The beatings just keep coming, don't they?

Even though Liam and I had already shared a date and one hot kiss that practically melted my—

Could we please keep things rated PG, please? I can hear every word.

I hadn't been going to say whatever Leo's mind had dredged up—the gutter, obviously. I'd been going to say that Liam had practically melted my lipstick off that night. Even so, I hadn't expected to see him until our date on Friday evening. He was supposed to be out of town at some law enforcement convention.

Well, it's obvious he decided to skip out of said convention. Oh, well. We gave it the good old gung ho try. It looks like we'll have to stay home, after all. I'll meet the two of you back inside once you've driven off Mister Lipstick Melter.

"Not a chance," my mother muttered underneath her breath, giving a wiggle of her fingers that she had recovered with her gloves. "Raven, get rid of him. Now."

Or not. You don't want to ruin your chances with a man of his obvious talents, now do you? I vote for postponing our trip to the coven indefinitely. Who knows, we might not even need to go by then.

Liam opened the door to his truck, keeping the engine running. He was wearing a brown suede jacket that framed his shoulders perfectly, and matching cowboy boots that landed in the snow with a thud.

Who would have thought I'd ever fancy a man wearing a worn old pair of cowboy boots?

Not me. Oh. That was one of those rhetorical questions, wasn't it?

"Ms. Marigold, it's nice to see you again," Liam greeted my mother, his gaze taking in our black outfits. His follow up response wasn't a surprise. "Raven? Is everything okay here?"

It took me a moment to realize that both my mother and I looked either ready to attend a party hosted by Goths—trust me, it was plausible given my mother's dark lipstick—or we were on our way to rob a bank.

"Yes, yes," I responded, sounding more and more like Beetle ever since he'd hired himself. I cleared my throat, attempting to throw the question back his way instead of actually providing an answer. "And you? Did something happen at the convention to cause you to leave and return home early?"

"It's a long story." Liam cocked his head slightly to the side, presumably waiting to see if I'd offer up more information as to why I was clutching a woolen watch cap in my hand. "I'm sorry. I should have called before stopping over, but I wanted to see how Leo was doing before driving home."

Oh, Liam was racking up the points left and right. My heart warmed at his thoughtfulness, and I couldn't stop the smile from blossoming on my face.

I'll give him a full point for that one. That was pretty sly, throwing me in as an excuse to see you. Maybe I didn't give the man enough credit. Our local sheriff is secretly a stud muffin.

"I also have Dr. Jameson's number, should it turn out that you need it."

Point lost. Back to zero. I hate needles.

"That's so sweet of you, Liam." How did I go about sending Liam on his way when all I wanted to do was ship my mother back to the city, ignore the war I might have started with my ultimatum, and invite him in for some coffee? "We're, um, we're just—"

"Heading out," my mother chimed in, holding up her keys

as if that was some type of proof of our intent. "We've got somewhere to be."

"Has something happened?" Liam asked, concern written all over his handsome features.

Oh, it was becoming harder and harder to lie to him. Being the most terrible liar that I am, it was best to stick as close to the truth as possible.

"We need to go find...a missing family pet."

I swear, sometimes I don't know where you come up with this stuff.

The point being was that my explanation was the truth... stretched as it may be. I never, ever wanted to lie to Liam. That was not the way to start a relationship. Not that we had one. I mean, we were just dating. And that was not to say I didn't want something more serious when the time came, but these things shouldn't be rushed. Right?

Why me? Rosemary could have figured out another way to guide you through the supernatural realm. It didn't have to be me. Is she just torturing me from the grave?

"And we must be going," my mother practically sang as she hit the unlock button on her key fob. "It was nice seeing you again, Liam."

"Wait. Leo is missing? I'll help you search," Liam offered hastily, pointing his thumb behind him to his truck. "Hop in. I'm sure Leo didn't get too far, especially in this cold weather."

"Oh, I'm not talking about Leo," I quickly corrected Liam, stepping forward to reassure him that I hadn't lost my cat. I was glad that he wasn't wearing gloves so that I could reach out and hold his hand. "My mother's pet...sugar glider...was taken by...a family member. Um, who lives up in Windsor. So, we're going to take a drive up there and...steal him back."

My words wouldn't stop flowing, even though I could

visually see myself shoveling deeper the longer I went on while trying to make my reasoning sound legitimate.

What. Have. You. Done?

"Raven, dear, Liam doesn't want to get involved with our family drama." My mother's awkward laugh echoed throughout the snow-covered lawn. "And *steal* is a very harsh word. I'm sure me and my...aunt...will come to some sort of agreement. Without disturbing the peace, of course. No stealing involved."

He's going to end up arresting the both of you for your own good.

Where was Heidi when I needed her? I told you that I was a horrible liar, and this situation I'd found myself in was no exception. Heidi always managed to make lying seem so effortless. I realize that wasn't a compliment, but the woman did have her talents—a born New Yorker.

Sugar glider? Who in the supernatural realm would come up with something like a sugar glider under these circumstances?

I wish I could have come up with a reasonable explanation as to why I chose a sugar glider, but the closest thing I could think of to a fairy was a butterfly. And I couldn't use a butterfly for several reasons, one being they weren't really something one kept as pets and their lifespan was only a month or two—I remembered that tidbit from a documentary back when I was in elementary school.

So...you decided to come up with a hairy bat/squirrel hybrid that has winged arms and beady eyes? Am I missing something? Regina, did you drop her on the head as a baby?

That about sums up the error of my ways, but I was more concerned with Liam and the fact that he was staring at me and my mother as if he'd found himself in an alternate universe in some different dimension.

The fact that it was taking Liam so long to form a sentence told me just how deep that hole was I'd dug with my story. And somehow...our current situation went from bad to worse.

I didn't think that was even possible, but it takes a certain special kind of talent to dig ditches, too. It just wasn't a very viable sort of talent.

"In my experience, domestic disputes like this never end up on a good note, especially when it involves dark clothing and midnight runs to distant locations."

Look at that. The good ol' sheriff is right once again. Time to call it a night.

My mother began nudging me in the back with her keys, but she didn't have to capture my attention. I could see where this conversation was going, but I wasn't sure how to stop it.

Going? I thought we were going inside and calling it a night? What have you done?

"I'll go with you," Liam offered, rubbing his chin as he thought through the sugar glider predicament that I'd put forth. "Having a police presence might end up being beneficial, so I'll drive."

Sweet angel of death, deliver your blow swiftly. Raven, do you know if they let one smoke catnip in jail? It's not technically a controlled substance.

Thirteen

It was probably a good thing my mother was sitting behind me in Liam's truck so that I couldn't see how furious she was in light of our current circumstances.

It's good to know that you still have at least a tiny bit of common sense left. I thought you'd lost it back at the house. A sugar glider? What could you possibly have been thinking? I don't ever want to hear another word about my "goose" comment that I said in the heat of battle.

As you can see, Leo had decided to ride along for grins and giggles. I figured he was probably in the back seat with my mother remaining invisible. It might prove helpful if we did, in fact, recover Strifle. She would have to appear as a sugar glider to Liam. Leo could no doubt communicate that fact to her prior to Liam discovering my deception.

Why on earth would I sit next to your mother when she's in one of her moods? Plus, I wouldn't miss this inevitable chat and Liam's reaction for...well, I would for some exceptional premium organic catnip, but that's beside the point. I'm lying on the dash-board enjoying the warmth of the heat.

"I've heard about sugar gliders making nice pets, but I've never known anyone who actually owned one," Liam said right on cue. He leaned forward and turned the heat up just a smidge. We'd let quite a bit of the warm air inside the cab escape while my mother had climbed into the backseat. It probably would have been nice of me to offer her the front seat, but there was no way I was going to allow the two of them to sit side by side. "What is the little fellow's name?"

"Strifle," both my mother and I said in unison. Not that it mattered, but you should know that my tone was a bit softer than hers.

Do you blame her? We're taking a mere human in front of a crazed witch's coven to do battle. Chances are your precious sheriff isn't going to live to tell the tale. I give him one in five, and that's if he draws his firearm first.

"Interesting name. Listen, why don't you tell me why your aunt took Strifle, and then maybe I can figure out a way to smooth the situation over without anyone becoming upset to the point of a confrontation." Liam flipped on the turn signal, letting absolutely no one behind know that we were about to go onto the highway. His innate need to follow the letter of the law wasn't surprising, but I was too worried about Leo's crazed coven comment to fawn over Liam's sense of right and wrong. "Let's start with your aunt's name. I didn't even know Rosemary had a sister."

I try to forget that bit of knowledge myself. This is a fairly impressive hole you've dug in such a short period of time, Raven.

It was hard for me to swallow the lump in my throat. All I'd been doing was telling Liam lie after lie, and the moment that the truth was revealed was less than an hour away. What would the coven do when Liam figured out their secrets?

Turn him into a goat. Although, I still say the toad tale has a bit of truth to the story.

I curled my fingers into my palm so that I didn't reach out and try to knock Leo down onto the floor. He technically didn't even have to be in the truck. He could have easily transported to Windsor in the blink of an eye. Maybe that would be best so that he could do some reconnaissance.

Like I said, it's not often I'm rewarded with this type of entertainment. It would be a shame to skip out on the show.

"They were...what you might say...estranged," Regina responded without hesitation. I slowly exhaled, relieved that she'd stuck to the truth. "Aunt Rowena and my mother always had a tenuous relationship. It was one of the reasons my mother moved to Paramour Bay."

Paramour Bay wasn't nearly far enough away from Windsor, if you ask me.

"I've seen that happen with too many families in my line of work." Liam shook his head in sorrow at the lack of relationship Nan had with her sister. "At least you kept in contact with your Aunt Rowena throughout the years. Did the two of you have a falling out yourselves? Is that why she took your...sugar glider?"

I barely kept my forehead from pressing against the cold window in search of some relief for the onset of a sudden headache that wasn't so unexpected. Leo was either hacking up a hairball or choking out a laugh. I was betting on the latter.

"I'm going to be as honest as I can with you, Liam," Regina said, causing both me and Leo to sputter. Liam cast a worried gaze my way, but I covered up my slip with a cough. "Strifle is... special. She and her owner—which is me, obviously—have a very strong bond. It's not healthy for us to be separated, but there are certain people—Aunt Rowena, in this case—who are greedy."

It does make me wonder if Rowena isn't involved in some way, though my bet is on Angelica. That woman was always and probably still is a power hungry—

"Is Strifle worth a great deal of money?" Liam asked, expertly maneuvering the truck into the left lane without knowing he'd cut off Leo's most likely unflattering term for Warlock Bronach's new wife. "I can see why that would make sense, given that I'm sure sugar gliders probably fall into the exotic pet category."

Exotic? That's giving Strifle and her gang of merry misfits a bit too much credit, but who am I to judge? If Deputy Fife here only knew. Strifle will be moving on to the next world if I have to help her along myself. It would be a pleasure after that forest incident years back.

"I do appreciate you driving us to Windsor, but it's best if I speak with Rowena privately," my mother stressed, sounding pretty pleased with herself for having come up with a story that was relatively close to the truth if one overlooked the relationships involved. "If that doesn't work, I'll let you step in to see if you can talk some sense into her letting go of her scheme. How does that sound?"

My mother might have asked Liam for his opinion, but she wasn't *really* asking for his opinion. This little road trip was going to go her way, no matter what. It's how my mother worked, but I was used to her outwitting maneuvers.

"I can work with that," Liam responded with a half-smile, his doubt of her success rather clear. He gave me a wink once he settled back in his seat for the somewhat long drive. At least, it was long for me, considering I had to sit in the passenger seat while my mother bore holes into the back of my head. "How are you coming along in your search for part-time help?"

"Your what?"

I cringed when my mother's condemning inquiry came from the backseat.

This is better than movie night. Do you think we could stop for popcorn?

I looked sideways at Liam, who was mouthing *sorry* as he kept his steady gaze on the highway in front of him. He still had a hint of that charming smile, which was the sole reason I didn't smack him in the arm. It wasn't his fault that he didn't know I hadn't told my mother. After all, I had an advertisement in the glass door for the entire town to see. As for Leo, well, he was enjoying my discomfort dealing with my mother just a little too much.

"I made a New Year's resolution, Mom." I hadn't realized how stressed I was until Liam reached over the console and rubbed the back of my hand. He most likely did so out of regret for throwing me under the bus, but she'd been going to find out sooner or later. "I'm going to hire some part-time help at the tea shop. This way, I can run out for the occasional appointment without closing up the store. It will also free me up to take some time to come see you and Heidi in the city."

Just pointing out that you won't need to visit Heidi if she moves to Paramour Bay.

My mother technically couldn't argue with that sentiment. No one could run a business by themselves, at least not in retail. It was a lot of work to make sure the small tea shop stayed in business, especially with months like the one we were currently suffering through.

If it wasn't for Nan's old side business of offering remedies for minor afflictions, I might be out of business. Don't get me wrong, Nan had turned a very nice profit with her business plan as it stood, and she'd been kind enough to hand it down to me. I was still planning on expanding things to include gourmet coffee beans, grinders, and equipment for preparing high-end blends.

She handed me down as well, but I don't hear any thank yous for my contributions.

It was evident that I didn't tell Leo enough how much I valued his company, support, and friendship. Who knows where I'd be if he wasn't here to guide me? He was my anchor in this crazy life I'd been gifted with recently.

I guess so...and you buy me premium organic catnip on a monthly subscription now.

I couldn't help but grin at the way Leo went about saying that he loved being my fill-in familiar, too. Liam thought I was smiling at him, and that was okay. We'd made progress in this little road trip, which meant we were closer to our destination. Pretty soon, we'd have Strifle and be able to free her of her constraints.

It wasn't like I had my head in the sand. I understood the ramifications of bringing someone inside the shop who didn't know about the supernatural elements that existed in this world.

Were there times I made holistic blends with a touch of magic in the shop?

Absolutely.

I did a lot of the more complicated spells at home, and the easier ones at the shop. Doing so in the backroom with the enchanted beads to prevent someone from overhearing me couldn't have been more perfect. It was a win-win, and hiring part-time help would absolutely free up time for me to learn even more of my craft.

Or burn down the tea shop...whichever comes first.

"Your grandmother never hired outside help, Raven," my mother said in such a way that I couldn't miss her meaning. "I'm not so sure you need to take on such a giant responsibility yourself, either."

If it weren't for the "all the catnip in the world" comment made by Beetle, I would be in agreement.

"Is everything okay?" I asked Liam, noticing his frown as he glanced at the rearview mirror.

I even looked over my shoulder, but all I saw were numerous headlights from other vehicles. Liam didn't answer right away, but instead began monitoring the side mirror.

"Liam?"

"Yes, everything's fine." Liam shot me a reassuring smile, though I was still troubled at what had caused his agitation. "It's nothing. There seemed to be a vehicle that was tailgating us a bit too close, but the driver fell back a bit."

Could it be Merrick Bronach? No, that made no sense. He didn't know we were driving to Windsor, and it was doubtful that he'd be following us back to his hometown.

Unlike you, he has the whole astroprojection spell down pat.

I didn't want Liam to think I was too concerned about the subject of someone following us, so I continued the previous discussion. Besides, I'm sure my mother was now watching the vehicles behind us very closely.

"On a side note, Jack spilled the beans to Heidi about Beetle's upcoming retirement." There wasn't a chance behind those burning gates below that I was going to tell my mother about Beetle's interest in working at the tea shop. I had enough on my plate, and even I was still figuring out a way to turn down the man's offer. I'm pretty sure that job interviews weren't supposed to go that way. "Heidi is definitely interested in moving to Paramour Bay."

I thought I heard my mother say something along the lines of *what was that girl thinking*, but I hadn't been talking to her. We still had some time on our drive, and I wanted to talk to Liam—even if it meant doing so in front of my mother.

"I spoke with Jack at the convention," Liam informed me as he continued to drive and monitor the road. His focus on the task at hand allowed me to study his profile. Besides being a gentleman, believing in right or wrong and his loyalty to the town he served, he really was a very handsome man. "Jack worries quite a bit about Heidi living in the city unprotected."

"Technically, it should be the other way around," I responded with a laugh. Heidi was a force to be reckoned with, and she was city through and through. "Jack should really be worried about anyone that crosses that woman's path. She doesn't allow anyone to take advantage of her, and she always takes precautions wherever she goes. I still have muscle aches that never went back to normal after that one self-defense class she made me go to last year."

Liam and I continued to talk about various things, and I found that his birthday was coming up in a month. He wouldn't tell me his exact age, but I figured he was a few years older than me. The more the conversation wore on and the closer the tires on his trusty F150 brought us to our destination, I truly appreciated that my mother and Leo hadn't interrupted or made some wisecrack that ruined the time I'd been given with Liam.

Mom was no doubt planning a way to retrieve Strifle without Liam figuring out we were dealing with a historic coven of witches. She was the one who wanted to deal with the situation in this manner, so it fell on her ability to finagle our way without any of us being turned into toads. I want it noted that I was all for letting my proposed deadline pass without uttering another word, hoping beyond hope that the Windsor coven would do the same without setting my world on fire.

Um, Raven.

Liam was still talking about the latest changes the local pub had instituted—mainly karaoke—and how the additional entertainment was drawing in a younger crowd. Paramour Bay had a lot of elderly residents, though there was quite a few new families in the midst. There weren't a lot of twenty-something adults hanging around in our small town. They'd much rather party at the hotspots in the nearby city.

I was rather enjoying the conversation. Unfortunately, the way Leo had said my name told me that my enjoyment was coming to an end.

A dead end, if you want the truth.

It was hard to decipher Leo's meaning, especially since I couldn't physically see him. I had no way to take my cues from his body language, but it wasn't needed after I'd looked over my shoulder to see if my mother was the cause for Leo's concern.

I bet you never thought you'd wish for the day that it was your mother's meddlesome ways that caused you grief.

It couldn't have been that simple, could it?

Nope.

You see, ever so gradually a mist began to form in the back seat next to my mother—who looked quite horrified. Had this been any other place and time, I would have relished in my mother's astonishment at encountering an outer worldly spirit. Unfortunately, Mazie had decided to pay us a visit...right behind Liam's driver seat!

Fourteen

I warned you quite plainly. A person can get frostbite if he or she physically touches a ghost. Weren't you just saying how thankful you were for my guidance? Well, what good is my most excellent directions if you don't listen to them?

The tips of my fingers *had* gone numb the very moment I waved my hand into the mist, doing my best to prevent Mazie from making a full appearance. What could she want with me right this minute? Liam would no doubt wreck the truck upon setting eyes on a bona fide ghost, thus delaying our quest to save Strifle...and ending any chance of us having a second kiss.

You know, maybe Mazie scaring the bejeebers out of the good ol' sheriff isn't such a bad idea. We could kill two birds with one stone...not that I'm advocating the death of those particular feathery nuisances. They taunt me when I'm trying to nap during the weekdays, you know that, don't you?

"Is everything okay?" Liam asked, noticing that I was reaching in the back seat. He went to lean down to see what it was exactly that I was doing, but I rested my hand on his shoulder to stop him.

"Yes, yes," I responded, not giving two winks that I sounded like Beetle. "Of course, everything is okay. Why wouldn't it be? I was just patting Mom's leg to make sure she hadn't fallen asleep on us."

"I'm wide awake, Raven. Wide awake, and a bit heated."

Of course, she's wide awake. We have a hitchhiking ghost on board.

Not yet, we didn't, and I wanted to keep the rest of the drive apparition-free.

"Is this our exit?" I asked, purposefully drawing Liam's attention away from the back seat. I quickly grabbed my gloves and began waving them frantically at the mist behind Liam's seat, attempting to show my mother what she needed to do. I crossed my fingers that he wouldn't look in the rearview mirror, either. "The drive wasn't too bad, was it? We really appreciate you taking time out to help us get Strifle back. My poor mother has been beside herself with worry that Aunt Rowena might have sold Strifle off to the highest bidder."

Wait until the good ol' sheriff sees that it's Tinkerbell and not a sugar glider. I'd like to see you explain your way out of that one, not that your Oscar-winning performances haven't been convincing up to this point.

"It is a bit warm back here," my mother chimed in, a bit out of breath from apparently waving her own gloves over the area that Mazie was trying to occupy. "Do you think we could pop a window for a moment, Liam? You know old ladies and their hot flashes."

Doubtful.

Liam didn't hesitate, reaching for the button on his door that would crack the window just a hair. It was sweet of him to do as Mom had asked, but I wasn't so sure a bit of suction was going to keep Mazie from materializing. He also turned the heat down a notch before flipping on the turn signal so that we could take our exit.

Hey, that was the only saving grace of this whole trip! I want my heat back.

"No worries, Ms. Marigold," Liam said in what had to be false understanding, but I did give him credit for trying to make my mother comfortable. On the flip side, I was pretty sure I could hear Leo's teeth begin to chatter as the cold seeped into the cab of the truck as if we'd driven straight to the North Pole. "Raven, are we taking a left or a right?"

Left or right?

Yes, Raven. Should your potential second date turn left or right at the stop sign? I'm pretty sure your directions have a direct bearing on whether Friday night's date actually takes place.

Leo was just being cranky that he'd lost his supply of hot air.

The complications from this trip were mounting; however, Mazie's presence got top awards.

"Left," my mother cried out, sounding more and more like she was losing a fight with a chicken in the back seat. "Take a left."

Liam once again attempted to look over his shoulder, and I did the only thing I could—I hit him.

Wooowww. I was so not expecting you to assault the police at this point.

Leo's exaggerating. Liam was fine, just a little bit in shock. I mean, I didn't really *hit him*, hit him. More like I had kept my hand where it was and he ran his face into my fist.

I so want a replay of that...even his cheeks blubbered in slow motion. For the record, you did not keep your hand on his shoulder. It was more of a left jab.

Okay, I *might* have straightened my arm a bit, but it had

been for Liam's own good. Who knew how he'd react to seeing a ghost in the back of his truck?

"I am so sorry," I exclaimed with sincerity, squeezing his shoulder in comfort. "I didn't know you were going to turn around like that. Are you okay? I am so sorry."

You're a horrible person. Absolutely horrible. Beating your boyfriend is not the answer.

Leo was right, but I would have to ruminate over that truthful tidbit later. Right now, I had to deal with the fact that a troubled spirit was attempting to appear next to my mother while she tried to give Liam directions to a house that we had no idea of its location.

"Ms. Marigold, is everything okay?" Liam asked with true concern this time. There was nothing I could do to stop his gaze from being pulled to the rearview mirror as if his dark eyes were magnets. "Do you need me to stop for a minute?"

I rested my right elbow next to the window and placed my hand over my eyes in humiliation. I couldn't watch this tragic event unfold. Liam would never ever again look at me the same way he did on New Year's Eve when the clock had struck midnight. Our relationship was over before it ever really began. Why did I have the worst luck with men? Especially the ones I liked?

That list is rather long. Where would you like me to start? I'm sure Heidi and I can gather together an intervention and spitball a strategy for you going forward.

"Everything is fine, Liam," my mother replied in a not so panic-stricken manner as before. She even cleared her throat as if the question was uncalled for. "You can roll the windows up now that we've all had some fresh air."

Well, that was anticlimactic. I had a bet on how many rollovers we were going to do during the crash.

I practically sighed with relief knowing that Mom had somehow gotten Mazie to give up her persistent attempt to join us on this trip. One thing was for sure. I was either going to have a heart attack at the young age of thirty or I was going to develop ulcers and have to give up coffee—I wasn't sure which was worse. After all, Mazie was drinking tea on the other side. There had to be coffee there, right?

Wait. Are you suggesting that they might not have my premium catnip in stock? That would definitely change the way we're going at this thing, you know.

"You can certainly pack a left," Liam muttered good-naturedly, rubbing his jaw tenderly as he brought the truck to a halt at the stop sign. There was a sparkle to his dark gaze that told me our date on Friday night was still on the schedule. "I'll have to remember that I need to bring some head gear on our date."

All the good ol' sheriff had to do was ask Ted. Do you remember when you hurled an energy ball at that giant and it smacked him right in the chest like a wrecking ball? I think he was sporting a dent in his wax for a week. By the way, I love that wrecking ball song. Miley is so tuned in.

Liam promptly rolled up the windows, though he didn't turn the heat up any higher than the midrange setting.

I always get overlooked. We could be in your mother's car with heated seats if you hadn't messed up with your award-winning story. Oh, and we could have left the police officer out of our little B&E we're doing later this evening.

Leo was being a nonstop chatterbox, and I was honestly getting a bit worried about him. Just how many of those catnip edibles had he consumed since we'd left the house?

Unfortunately, Leo didn't answer.

"After you make a left, you'll go about a mile or two until

you see a small neighborhood on your right. It's a gated community, but the guard isn't on duty at this time of night. I know the code, so access won't be a problem," my mother said, once again surprising me with the knowledge she possessed. "We should also go over the plan. I'd like the three of you—I mean, the two of you—to remain in the truck while I go inside and speak to my aunt to work things out."

Gated community? Code? Since when did my mother visit Aunt Rowena?

Raven?

My concern for Leo mounted, but we had more pressing issues that had to be dealt with first. Was Mom really going to see Aunt Rowena? Or was Mom just using Aunt Rowena as an excuse to locate the temple where Merrick and his cronies had Strifle hidden? It was difficult for me to figure out what plan needed to be executed.

"Mom, are you sure that I shouldn't go inside with you?" I asked, shifting in my seat so that I could see my mother's expression. There was just enough brightness from the red light that I could see her pursed lips and her narrowed eyes. "We wouldn't want Aunt Rowena to think that you're all alone in this endeavor, would we?"

Yoo-hoo. Raven.

"That's not such a bad idea, Ms. Marigold." Liam gained points for backing me up in this moment. "It's obvious that you and your aunt don't have the best of relationships. She wouldn't have stolen your...um, sugar glider...had she not wanted to hurt you in some way. Raven's presence might help alleviate any tension that might suddenly develop."

Is there a reason we're pulling up to a wrought iron gate that looks like something out of a movie studio's set for a horror movie?

Great. Leo's short-term memory loss had kicked in with a

bang, right when we didn't have time for another problem. Hopefully, something jogged his memory soon. The last thing we all needed was for him to suddenly materialize on the dashboard of Liam's truck and hack up a hairball.

Mom wasn't the only one having hot flashes.

Hmpfh. Me, too.

The stress of hiding being a novice witch was overwhelming, but Leo's wave of welcomed warmth came from the fact that Liam had turned up the heat when he rolled down the driver's side window in order to punch in the code.

We'd finally arrived.

I feel like I should say "to our summary execution", but I'm not sure exactly why. Raven? Is there something I should be worried about? Where are we?

Considering that I had no idea if Mom had any real intention of dropping in on Aunt Rowena, Leo had every right to worry. On top of that, the only tension that I could envision increasing was my own while we figured out a way to break into the coven's temple—which was no doubt protected by a whole litany of very powerful warding spells and glyphs.

Did you say temple? As in...ohhhh, it's starting to come back to me. Raven, I'm not feeling so good about this.

"We're here," Liam announced needlessly as he glanced in the rearview mirror. Guilt, along with the cold air, began to wash over me. I should have somehow told Liam that it wasn't wise to come with us, for now I was bringing a human into a witch's spell combat. "No guard, just like you said. I'll punch the code in for you, Ms. Marigold."

This is it. We're all going to be turned into toads.

Fifteen

"Mom, this is really evolving into a seriously bad idea," I whispered, walking side by side with her down the sidewalk. "Liam is going to figure out that we're not just visiting our auntie's house, and then he's going to follow us into this place to make sure everything is okay. And in case you hadn't noticed...it's not going to end well!"

I was panicking just a little, but I gave myself permission considering we were basically inside a witch neighborhood to steal back an abducted fairy from a sacred temple with an armed human official in tow.

When you put it like that, I'd be more than happy to stay in the truck to keep an eye on him. I mean, for safety's sake.

"Breathe, Raven. Now is not the time to lose your nerve," my mother stated, seemingly oblivious to the cold. "This house is as good as any."

I wasn't sure what Mom meant by this particular house being as good as any, but it wasn't like I had the choice to abandon her plan for this rescue party. Breathing didn't help any, either. In fact, all it did was make my nose numb and give me the sensation that I needed to cough. I'd definitely give our position away then. That wouldn't be the best of ideas, considering that someone might hear me. The way my luck was going, they'd hurl a fireball and turn us into cinders.

You don't need to cough, Raven. That light irritation in your chest was a small current of energy that is hanging in the air. I hate to break this to you, but we've already been made.

Leo's warning had me coming to an abrupt halt, but my mother seemed to know my intention before my feet stopped moving. She clasped a hand around my wrist and practically dragged me up a small sidewalk that had been cleared of snow. It was like they'd been anticipating our arrival.

I couldn't help but look around us to see if there were witches and warlocks lining up to hit us with some horrible spell that would have us all turning into toads, only to have us freeze to death out here in the bitter cold temperatures. I realized that the sound I was hearing was my own heartbeat, the blood rushing through my ears a little too rapidly.

That's the engine, Sherlock. The engine on the truck that I should be inside of where it's warm and safe.

Leo was right. I was hearing the idling of the truck, which only reminded me that Liam was probably keeping a very close eye on our trek to the front porch of some stranger. Only Mom didn't take the two wooden steps up to the porch. No, she chose to go around the side of the house. To anyone looking, particularly Liam, it would seem we were going around to either a side or back entrance.

"If I remember correctly, the temple is located in the center of the neighborhood." Mom finally dropped my arm, and I continued to foolishly follow without thought. "We need to walk about three blocks, but we can take a shortcut through the backyards."

I'm not going to lie. Watching my mother move ahead of me at a brisk pace dressed as a cat burglar had me believing I may have taken a hit of Leo's catnip. The black leather needed to be thrown into a dumpster behind the tea shop, never to be seen again. It wasn't that she didn't look good in leather, but that was the problem. I shouldn't have to see my mother looking like she could jump small buildings, save the world, and attract the attention of a new boyfriend at the same time. It just wasn't right.

What have you done? I can't get that image out of my head now! Yuck!

"Leo thinks the council already knows we're here," I said, wondering why I even bothered. My mother could also hear every comment Leo uttered, so she was well aware of the small exchanges going on between Leo and me. "Why would they allow us to break into the temple? It doesn't make any sense."

Nothing about this ill-conceived rescue mission makes sense. I think there's an icicle hanging from my nose.

"They know we're here, but I cast a spell that makes it seem we're coming from the back of the neighborhood. All of the council's resources will be spent at the back gate, giving us a chance to see inside the temple before they converge." My mother held up a hand as if we were members of S.W.A.T. To her credit, it worked. I came to a complete stop when we were about to cross another road. "We should only have to worry about one or two witches or warlocks left behind to guard the temple."

"I hope you realize that we're overdue for a very long...and I mean, very long...conversation."

My mother had spent her entire life shielding me from witchcraft, and here she was performing it like it was second nature.

Actually, it has everything to do with nature, but I see your point. Your mother has been holding out on us. I'm rather offended. Is it odd that I want to share this new information with Ted? Hmmm. I wonder if this means I'm beginning to think of him as a friend rather than a henchman. I shall ponder that while smoking my catnip pipe should we not end up as toads later tonight.

"I had no choice but to have your grandmother believe that I'd left that life behind. I actually did, with an occasional spell here and there to keep my hand in the mix." My mother began to proceed through the next yard of a house that was completely dark. The homeowner had been wise to go to bed this early. It's where I should be instead of biting off more than I could chew. I was so going to end up being a toad. "But as I said the other day, witchcraft is not something you forget. It never leaves you. I'd hoped for you to avoid having to live with such a curse. Seeing you struggle every day isn't easy for me."

Had my mother just made this moment about us?

Maybe it's the effect of the curse that's about to descend upon us. We're dealing with evil creatures, Raven. They're giving you something you've always wanted, only to have it croak away for all eternity.

Leo's awful pun didn't erase the fact that my mother was attempting to right a wrong. Maybe I was being too optimistic, but I'd looked forward to this moment. I just wish it hadn't come at a time when we were about to commit a crime against the coven and die.

"There it is," my mother whispered before I could reply to her previous admission of guilt over how she'd handled things with Nan and me. "I'm going to need some of your energy, Raven. Hold out your hand."

I'd slipped on my gloves when we'd gotten out of the truck,

but my mother had quickly whipped one off of my left hand without hesitation. She must have taken her own glove off earlier, for we were now holding hands. Not once had heat radiated through the palm of my right hand, which told me that my mother might very well have been successful in diverting the council's attention to the back of the neighborhood.

We're dealing with professionals here, Raven. They'll strike without warning. Your powers are useless here. Why, oh why, did I agree to go fairy hunting? I mean, of all things, a flipping fairy! What had I been thinking?

Leo could join the club, because this night wasn't going anywhere near the way I'd planned. It would have been better for all of us to have let my ultimatum slide into oblivion.

And have Mazie haunt you for the rest of your life? Great plan.

True, but I'm sure I could have located a spell to have kept her on the other side. None of that mattered now. We were here at the temple, and it was only a matter of time before my mother found us a way in.

Or not. Is that who I think it is?

Angelica was bundled up in a red dress coat and matching scarf. I wasn't one to give fashion advice, but the two reds clashed enough to make a woman wince.

"Mom?" I whispered, squeezing her hand and hoping that she was paying attention. She'd been muttering a chant underneath her breath that wasn't doing a lick of good. "Mom, do you see—"

"Yes, Raven. Now let me finish."

Sure enough, my mother took another minute to complete whatever invocation she'd been casting out to prevent anyone guarding the temple from locating our presence. It was foolish to think they would fall for it, especially considering a spell against a spell was like a catch-22. With that said, I could literally feel the energy from the earth travel through the soles of my black knee-high boots, into my body, and out through the palm of my hand to enhance my mother's power tenfold.

I believe your mother is just gaining us some time to retrieve the package. That warlock is very, very powerful. Merrick Bronach won't be deceived for long.

I was more worried about the fact that Angelica had entered the temple without exception. Mom had mentioned breaking and entering, but the front door was apparently unlocked. Maybe this was going to be easier than we all thought.

A witch's temple is just like a church, Raven. What good would it serve to have the door closed to its faithful followers?

That made total sense, but it still didn't explain why Mom thought we'd be breaking and entering into the temple.

There's a very powerful spell that is being used to prevent human beings from entering the sanctity of the shrine. Get it? Breaking...then entering?

It appeared that I had been worried over nothing. We weren't technically committing a crime, but the punishment of being turned into a toad was still viable. We needed to get in and out of the temple—with Strifle in hand—as quickly as possible.

At least ten minutes had passed since we'd left Liam sitting in his truck. How long did we have before he came looking for us? What would happen if he decided to knock on the front door of the house that we had feigned entrance into as if it were Aunt Rowena's residence?

"Angelica isn't where the council believes her to be, which tells me that she's the guilty party," my mother surmised, nodding her head as if she'd just solved the mystery. Had she? Could it be that simple? Maybe we'd be able to make it back to Liam before he became too curious about our where-abouts. "Angelica must have Strifle locked up somewhere inside the temple, and now she has no choice but to remove the evidence to prevent the coven from discovering her deception."

"Remove the evidence?" The way my mother had phrased the last part of her statement seemed a bit dire. "I know this is going to sound rather foolish on my part, but isn't that what we want? For Strifle to cross over to the other side?"

"Raven, Angelica isn't going to free Strifle from whatever confinement vessel she's been placed in," my mother informed me as she began to walk toward the temple. I reluctantly followed. "Angelica will merely move the familiar to another hiding place, this time farther away from the coven so that they can't detect the distressed energy that Strifle must be emitting."

Strifle's pain and anguish sounded horrible. I'm pretty sure my sympathy for the little pixie was the only reason my legs allowed me to keep walking toward the door of the rather large church. I mean, it looked like a church with the tall steeple, although there was only a spire with no cross.

Don't let the outside appearance fool you.

"Stay one step behind me, Raven," my mother warned right as she opened the door. I fully expected warmth to envelop us, but there was absolutely no difference in the temperature. "Leo, I need you to keep watch for anyone or anything approaching the front doors."

Why do I always get to be the one to stand outside in the...

Leo's grumblings faded away as Mom and I stepped into a —get this—a dark and menacing forest. It was hard not to instinctively back up a step. And trust me, I tried. The door to the temple had already shut behind us, oddly leaving us still exposed to the outside elements.

"Mom," I whispered, not seeing anything or anyone else but the stark oak trees all around us. Strangely, there was a thin blanket of snow on the ground with several footprint paths all headed in one direction—forward. I couldn't help but glance upward. Sure enough, there was no ceiling. In its place was a full moon, shining its shadowy beams on the pathway in front of us. "Mom, what is this place?"

"The temple is nothing but a designation for where the coven comes together to show their appreciation for everything the earth provides for us." Mom gestured toward the shadowy footpath, but I wasn't so keen to go in that direction. The door behind me seemed like the better option. "The altar is that way. I'm betting Angelica has Strifle near the dais somewhere to disguise the energy."

How had everything fallen into place so perfectly? Was this rescue mission really going to be that simple? Why was my mother helping me as if she'd never expressed her discontent with the life I'd chosen to lead?

I fully expected Leo to answer me, but he'd gone back outside to stand watch. Not having him reply to my questions was rather similar to when his short-term memory decided to kick in—I didn't like it.

Leo was my sounding board, but he could also be rather knowledgeable in times like these. He provided a background for these new discoveries. One would have thought having my mother here to guide me would have been just as good, but without Leo by my side...I was a bit lost.

If my past experiences with two dead bodies and one resolved fifty-three-year-old murder were anything to go by, nothing was ever as it seemed. Was Angelica really responsible for preventing Strifle from crossing over into the afterlife? Maybe that was the reason Merrick Bronach had been so proactive in his bid to stop me from investigating.

The crunching of the snow seemed to echo throughout the trees, but my mother didn't slow down in the least. Instead, she quickened her pace and it wasn't long before a clearing emerged with an ancient gnarled oak tree in the middle of a wide opening as if no one dared to go near it.

Its power was undeniably strong.

"There," my mother whispered, pointing with a bare finger toward Angelica. The woman's red coat was easily seen drifting behind her as she disappeared behind the thick trunk of the old oak tree. "We need to follow her. She'll lead us straight to Strifle."

Before either my mother or I could take a step forward, someone reached out of the darkness and dragged us back into the shadows.

Sixteen

"What are the two of you doing here?" Angelica asked us once she released us from those long red nails of hers. "Do you realize what you've done?"

I couldn't help but look back over my shoulder, knowing one hundred percent that I'd seen this woman walk around the ancient tree as if she were a mirror image. How had she pulled a stunt like that?

I know, I know.

You don't have to say it.

She's a witch, but I hadn't seen her use any spells, which had me one breath away from really freaking out. Even the simplest forms of cantrips require some sort of verb, material, or somatic component. I hadn't seen her move her lips, gesture oddly with her hands, or produce a material object that precludes everything but an enchanted item. I was beginning to realize just how far we were behind the eight ball.

"Wait just a second," Angelica said rather cautiously, taking a step back and holding up her right hand as if she'd touched a snake. She pointed a long, extended finger directly at my mother. "You're Regina Lattice Marigold."

My mother tilted her chin a little higher in acknowledgment, almost taunting the older woman to try something.

"Mom, I don't want to be a toad. Compel her or something," I muttered, using my elbow to jab her in the side. The black leather coat she had on cushioned my poke, but I'd done it with enough force to knock her off balance. "Angelica, we know that you have Strifle. Mazie isn't going to rest until her familiar is released to continue her journey to her next destination."

"Raven, we told you when you made your unannounced visit that we had nothing to do with that pesky pixie going missing." Angelica might have answered me regarding Strifle, but her slanted eyes remained focused on my mother. "I remember when you last visited here, wanting answers that your mother wouldn't give you. It seems as if history repeats itself, now doesn't it?"

Don't get me wrong. I was well aware that my mother had visited the coven looking for answers when she was a teenager, but I hadn't realized it had been because my grandmother had purposefully kept details of our family history from my mother. After all, Nan had left behind a ton of boxes full of papers and journals about our ancestors. She hadn't seemed to want to hide anything from me.

"My reasoning for visiting the council all those years ago had everything to do with my father and nothing to do with a crime committed against one of our own." Regina very deliberately took a step forward, clearly not afraid of Angelica. I happened to disagree with that rather hazardous assumption. Then again, the palm of my hand produced not one ounce of energy. Was Angelica really not a threat to our safety or that of

Strifle? "I found no answer then, but my daughter and I fully intend to right a wrong against Mazie Rose Young—a member of this coven. Now, what has been done with Strifle?"

It was well known that the falling out between Nan and Aunt Rowena had been over a man, and it had always been assumed that the male in question had been my mother's biological father. Apparently, the answer lies somewhere with someone in this coven—the same coven we were about to go to battle with.

"Mom?" I wanted to remind her that we were outnumbered, and not by a slim margin. We'd been found, and it would be wise to retreat before the others arrived. "Mom, we need to leave."

I couldn't have been the only one to notice the gust of wind that had come out of nowhere, managing to change the stark quality of the cold air. There was a threatening sense of vulnerability that hadn't been there before. Had something happened to Leo? Was there someone else nearby, listening to our conversation?

Had Angelica set us up or was she just waiting for reinforcements?

My mother was too busy studying the woman to hear a word I said, which was rather unsettling. I began to run through a list of the few spells I'd memorized for times like this, but only one came to mind effortlessly...and it wasn't an invocation.

The longer this dragged out, the faintest beginnings of tingles began to warm the palm of my hand. I'd only ever lost control over the energy that I'd absorbed into my body once, and it had almost cost Ted his life. I was grateful that my right glove was still encasing my hand, and I even clutched the glove my mother had removed to prevent myself from doing some serious harm.

"Mom, we need to hurry this up," I murmured, wondering why Leo wasn't getting any sense of our troubles. My mother's intention to follow Angelica to Strifle had been great, but it had been a bad idea to separate the group. Maybe that's where the sense of vulnerability came from. "We need to find Leo. Now."

I'm here! I think they're headed this way, and—

Leo was in his physical form when I finally set eyes on him running toward us with his tail all puffy. If I were honest with you, it was more of an erratic hop instead of an all-out run.

What are you doing talking to the gold-digger? "I beg your pardon?" Angelica exclaimed, resting her hand over her red scarf. The two drastically different shades of red were still bothering me, but clearly there were more important things to worry about than coordinating our clothes. "I will have you know that I love Merrick Bronach very much. He's a visionary of our time. A powerful warlock who had been deprived of his seat on the council for far too long simply because of politics."

Ew. Yuck. Don't they have someone to clean up around here?

At first, I thought Leo was describing his thoughts on Merrick Bronach. That wasn't the case. A large black insect had been crawling across the tip of my boot, and it was headed straight for Leo. With one smack, he'd sent the six-legged insect sailing through the air.

I couldn't suppress my shudder of disgust, but my mother was oblivious to anything but what Angelica had to say about Merrick Bronach.

"The Merrick who I once knew never wanted anything to do with the council," Regina said with a shake of her head. "What changed?"

Is your mother seriously having an old home moment right now while an entire coven of witches is descending on us? We need to skedaddle while we still can. Right now!

"What changed?" Angelica asked, as if she hadn't heard my mother correctly the first time. "Everything. This coven has disintegrated in the ensuing years, and the only one who has been able to keep it from falling apart into total anarchy has been my dear husband."

I couldn't help but look for any more six-legged creatures, but I was also very careful not to trip over a tree root as I scanned the ground. The temple, or whatever these witches wanted to call this displaced wood, was nothing like I'd imagined. It was dark, damp, and eerily quiet. The earth I received energy from was vibrant and alive...not dark or evil.

Then call up one of those little incantations to stop your mother from setting up some type of group therapy for the coven! It took you weeks to memorize three of them well enough to use them offensively.

Four, but I wasn't about to argue with Leo when Strifle still needed to be located and rescued from whatever prison the coven had trapped her in these past few months.

"What do you mean the coven is disintegrating?" Regina asked with what sounded like true sincerity.

That's from the acting class your mother had when she was six. Don't buy it. I've seen it all before. Regina is buying you time to cast one of those emergency spells I made you memorize.

"No, I'm not," my mother snapped, shutting down Leo's best efforts at having me try to get us out of here unscathed. "Raven, don't you do a thing until we get the information we've come here to get. Don't you see? If the coven is disintegrating, the council would have the very motive for taking Strifle. They need her power."

The same coven who is closing in on the temple right this minute! I won't make it too far as a toad!

"I'm going to say this one more time," Angelica exclaimed with irritation as she looked over her shoulder. The air was beginning to shift all around us. The brightness of the moon seemed to dim, and the bark on the trees became almost black. We were running out of time, but why did Angelica seem to want us out of harm's way? "The council did *not* take Strifle. As for the reason the coven is disintegrating, you have no need to look any further than your own family. Rosemary's excommunication caused a huge rift, and it's only gotten worse over the years. No one wants the inconvenience of the council's oversight or the tax."

Toads don't have the ability to smoke catnip in a pipe, you know.

Leo was still stuck on the fact that the council might exact revenge like one of the old witch's tales, but I was beginning to believe Angelica was telling the truth. What if the council wasn't responsible for Strifle's disappearance?

"Are you saying that there is a war brewing between the two factions?" My mother rarely showed when something knocked her off balance, but her amazement upon hearing such news was evident. She slowly shook her head, but it wasn't in an effort to say she didn't believe Angelica. It was more that she was beginning to realize how catastrophic a war could be between the divided witches. I agreed with her, because the ones who could get hurt the worst were the human bystanders—like Liam. "Are the council members in danger of losing their seats? Are you? Don't answer that. I don't want to know. Raven and I want no part of any war, but are you suggesting that the other faction might have Strifle?"

Oh, I can see where this is going a mile away. And I really would rather be miles away from here when your mother figures out who is leading the other side, so can we go now? Please?

"Angelica, who's leading the opposing faction?" my mother asked cautiously, taking a step back so that we were side by side. She even grabbed my hand, but it wasn't the one without the glove. "Give us a name."

"Rowena, of course. Your mother's sister."

Raven, I'll see you at home. I can find out how all this ends another time, and I really need a hit or two of my catnip after ingesting all of this new information. My acid reflux is acting up. I don't suppose I could trouble anyone for a saucer of milk, no?

It wasn't surprising to see Leo vanish into thin air, but I'd come to know that he usually didn't go far in times of crisis. He just hid behind his ability to cloak himself.

Why are you giving away my secrets? I was serious about my acid reflux. Maybe I have an ulcer. You have caused a lot of stress in my life. I should seek compensation.

I couldn't worry about Leo right now, especially when my mother had a death grip on my hand. It was a wonder my fragile bones didn't crack under the pressure.

"Ever since Rowena took in that boy, she's been spouting hearsay about the coven's rules being too strict," Angelica shared, shaking her head in aversion to such a proclamation. I wasn't sure what boy she was talking about, and I wasn't given a second to ask. Angelica was speaking rather rapidly now, and I realized we didn't have long before our chances of getting out of here went from slim to none. "Nearly half the coven is on your aunt's side, and the others remain faithful to Merrick, though some are only loosely affiliated. I was here to check on the artifacts due to the alarm being sounded. We were all assigned posts. Attacks on the neighborhood have happened a lot recently, which always seems to coincide with an invaluable relic going missing. Merrick and I decided to set a trap, but that's when I realized you'd snuck into the temple for other reasons."

You might want to take a step back. There's that giant bug again.

I quickly retreated, this time not looking behind me. It had been instinct to separate myself from anything with six legs. Not even my mother's hold on my hand could stop me from losing my balance and landing on my backside.

It might not have been my most graceful moment, but my tumble to the ground gave me a different vantage point...and also had me solving our latest case.

Seventeen

"Mom, I know who has Strifle!" I managed to get to my feet, wiping away as much snow and wetness as I could before grabbing her arm. "We need to—"

It was clear that someone had entered the temple from the resounding boom that echoed throughout the trees. It was too late to stay out of sight from the rest of the coven, regardless of the fact that Angelica had warned us to leave minutes earlier. We were about to be caught red-handed, but I had a bargaining chip.

It better be one of those gold chips they can use at the casino, because otherwise they're going to turn us into toads and then fry us in a pot of boiling lard. We'll be turned into fried toad chips.

"Follow my lead," I muttered, practically dragging my mother into the moonlight on the path so that there was no mistaking our whereabouts. Sure enough, Merrick and the two remaining members on the council were marching our way. I made sure to announce our intentions. "We come in peace!"

Wait a second. Why didn't you tell me we were trying to pass ourselves off as aliens?

"What is going on here?" Merrick called out in impatience, his gaze searching behind us. No doubt, he was seeking out his wife. His concern for her welfare was evident. "Angelica? Are you alright, my dearest?"

"Yes, sweetheart." Angelica walked past us through the thin layer of snow with her head held high, taking her rightful place next to her husband. Ruby and Hestia were standing on the other side of him, completing the council. "I found them here, looking for Mazie Rose Young's familiar. I tried once again to tell them we had nothing to do with such an evil injustice."

Ohhhh, she's good. Oscar-worthy. Angelica might take home the award this year, Raven. She did much better than you did earlier with that lackluster story.

"Raven, who has Strifle?" my mother asked underneath her breath as Angelica continued to divulge to Merrick all that had taken place here tonight. "We need to finish this up quick before they decide to put us on trial for violating the sanctity of the temple."

Trial? I don't do well in high stressful situations, Raven. I'll end up rolling on both of you for a lighter sentence. Sorry.

We didn't tamper with anything, but I couldn't worry about what Merrick and his cronies might or might not decide to do to us. Angelica hadn't mentioned once that she'd informed us of the coven's inner struggles. Her glaringly obvious silence on that subject told me that she didn't want her husband to know she'd disclosed such privileged information.

"Regina Lattice Marigold, is that you?" Merrick asked, stepping forward in total disbelief. Angelica made sure she kept a hold of his arm. It wasn't because the man was in his late seventies, either. Truthfully, he looked at least ten years younger and quite spry, especially in that long black—and presumably very expensive—dress coat. Why was it that men always seemed to age in a more distinguished manner than women? "It's been years. I can't believe it's you."

We're not going to age another day if you don't get us out of this mess your mother got us into. Dealing with more than one of you is more than I can handle at the moment. I have a contract, you know. I was made certain promises—legal binding promises.

"I can't believe that you would want to take away our progress and go back to the old ways," my mother exclaimed in anger, totally outing Angelica. So much for finishing this up quickly. I understood Mom's reasoning for calling out Merrick, especially considering that the deep-rooted coven rules were the exact reason Nan had been shunned from this community to begin with. "If you're the one responsible for detaining a familiar from crossing over to the afterlife, I demand you hand her over this minute. Does the fifth council member have her?"

Oh, yeah. I forgot about the fifth member. I guess that must seem rather important now. So, I'll tell you now—there's a fifth council member.

That would have been useful information, but it had come a little too late.

"No," Merrick replied angrily, his previous softening evaporating upon my mother's accusations. "We have not—nor would we ever—resort to kidnapping to get our way. Not even the other faction would stoop to those levels."

The warlock has a point. There are rules.

"Someone in this coven has Strife in some type of binding spell to prevent her from leaving this realm."

A point has been added to your mother's side of the scoreboard.

"I repeat, no one on this council nor any of our members whom are still in good standing would do anything so atrocious."

No point for reiteration. The score remains one to zero.

"No one ever would have ever foreseen this coven would be split into two factions, but the council hasn't prevented that outcome, has it?" Regina asked, taking the proverbial stick and poking the bear. In this case, four very powerful and hungry bears. "Show us the fifth council member. Should the witch or warlock prove to us that this council is innocent, then we will seek out Aunt Rowena. No familiar should be used as a tool in this nonsense war that you've created."

While Leo continued to keep score, I'd been watching the other three participants closely. The inherent instinct that usually came over me had settled itself in my stomach, and I was ninety-nine percent positive who the guilty party was within the suspect pool as we knew it. The other one percent came from not knowing about a fifth council member existing.

"May I speak?"

You don't need to. Just apologize for the intrusion, and maybe they'll let us be on our way.

"Show yourself," Merrick demanded of Leo.

Everyone's attention had been on Merrick Bronach and my mother, but their focus had immediately turned to Leo when he poked his head out from behind one of the trees lining the path. I didn't want anyone's attention on the fact that Nan had dabbled in black magic. That little tidbit would only solidify their opinion on the fate of the Marigold family.

Raven, do something. They're staring at me like they're going to eat me. I'm not that tasty.

I'd always been a horrible public speaker, and now was no exception. The palms of my hands began to perspire, and I took off my right glove to buy myself some time. What if I was wrong? What if Aunt Rowena was the criminal mastermind and I was about to accuse an innocent woman?

166

I don't have *time!*

"Warlock Bronach, the witch who has bound Strifle to this realm is the same witch who has been stealing the sacred artifacts from your temple," I declared, not surprised when my mother began rubbing the back of her neck to ease her tension. This was either going to go well or we were definitely going to end up as toads. At least my announcement had the four council members looking away from Leo. "I stand before you to declare that I believe—"

"Oh, get on with it," Angelica interrupted, apparently not a fan of my public speaking, either. "Who is it you believe has been stealing from our sacred temple?"

The fact that Angelica didn't mention Strifle and the fairy's plight told me that Mazie had been correct in dubbing the woman a gold-digger. Angelica didn't care about anything other than power and affluence within the coven. Mazie had been spot on with the other nicknames she'd given, and I believe there was only one moniker my beloved ghost had gotten wrong.

"Hestia Calixta!"

Evidently, I wasn't too bad at giving public speeches.

I've seen better, but your announcement definitely got their attention off yours truly, which is fine by me.

I had even been able to instigate a long chorus of "ohs" that were carried out in unison. The only problem I could foresee was that Hestia wasn't going to give up so easily. She was *not* clueless.

"I beg your pardon?" Hestia replied, using her elbow to

prompt Ruby into backing up whatever story that was about to be concocted. "Ruby, tell them they're being ridiculous!"

My heartrate has calmed down a bit. I think we're good. There's no need to rush me to the vet—not that I'd ever set a paw in Dr. Jameson's veterinarian clinic. Not in this lifetime or the other eight.

Leo definitely didn't have nine lives left by anyone's count. Who knows what Hestia might do to get out of this predicament? Unfortunately—and if I were right in my assumption—she was the only one who knew where Strife was being kept.

Hmmmm. I forgot all about that little pixie. See? That's what happens when I'm in fear of croaking for all eternity.

"It all makes sense," I said forcefully, not letting go of my mother's hand in case we needed to defend ourselves. I'd been so nervous about being caught that the cold air no longer felt so chilly. "The sacred artifacts in the temple are being stolen, but which ones? Have you ever thought to narrow down their specific powers?"

I didn't know you were such a gambler, Raven. You better hope you're right on the money with this one.

I wasn't usually a risk taker, but it was rather empowering to have Mom by my side. There was no doubt that she was watching and waiting for any sign of attack. She wouldn't allow us to be blindsided by the council.

Really? Then where is the fifth council member, huh?

My mother's lips twitched in irritation at Leo's constant interference. In an odd way, his quips kept me balanced.

Merrick and Angelica were whispering to each other in doubt while Ruby continued to stare at Hestia with suspicion. Their distraction gave me time to glance over my shoulder, just to confirm that there was no one behind us. The oversized looming tree that was surrounded by an old wooden bench covered with a dusting of snow were the only items in sight.

Don't get distracted, Raven. You've got them biting, now set the hook. Become the angler I always knew you can be.

"When these so-called attacks Angelica mentioned took place on the neighborhood and all of you were defending the coven, did any of you do so with Hestia by your side?" I asked, forcing the other three members to recall Hestia's whereabouts. I even took my questions a bit further. "Who was the one who found Mazie's body when she died of natural causes?"

Another collective round of "ohs" and "ahs" made their rounds, and I was quite proud of myself to have solved this mystery. Unfortunately, we still didn't have Strifle in our possession. Technically, I wasn't sure what would happen once we located Strifle.

Don't worry. We don't have to kill the pesky sprite, if that's what you're thinking.

It was, but I had more pressing issues to worry about—especially when Hestia suddenly stepped forward with enough anger radiating off her that the palm of my hand instantly reacted. The only thing that prevented my arm from involuntarily raising was my mother's vise-like grip.

"How dare you accuse me of such a thing!" Hestia exclaimed, shaking her finger at me as if I were caught sullying her favorite teakettle. "Ruby, tell them that I was with you. Go ahead. Tell them!"

Hestia's not so clueless after all, is she?

"Ruby, do the right thing. Tell us the truth," I encouraged, recalling the redhead's expression the night I'd been able to astroproject myself into their council meeting. The woman might be opinionated, but she wasn't a bad person. With enough prompting, she should do the right thing. "Strifle is in tremendous pain being trapped here. It isn't fair that she be kept from crossing over to be with Mazie. Be honest with the council members, Ruby. Tell them that Hestia was worried about the vision of her own death. Explain to them that she was stealing artifacts to help prevent the fateful vision from coming true, and that her heinous plan was preventing Strifle from crossing through the veil all because Hestia wanted to use the fairy's power to avoid the inevitable."

Not to make you feel bad or anything, but it is human nature to fight death.

"Is this true, Hestia?" Merrick demanded, patting Angelica's hand in reassurance that everything was going to be okay. "You should know that a vision could be years in the future. Stealing from the temple? Causing a familiar to be separated from..."

Merrick couldn't even finish his inquiry. He was too busy shaking his head in astonishment, hurt, and anger. Ruby was standing beside him wringing her hands in dismay, and Angelica seemed ready to put Hestia on trial immediately. I wasn't sure I wanted to know the punishment for these types of crimes.

"How could you do this to us, Hestia?"

"Where are those artifacts? You've weakened the coven with your treachery."

"I'm sorry, Hestia," Ruby declared painfully over the numerous questions being thrown Hestia's way. "Borrowing the artifacts from the library was one thing. But causing a familiar pain?"

Their voices began to carry over one another, though I could hear Leo's thoughts as clear as if he were inside my head.

Trust me, you don't want to know the punishment for one such crime, let alone the lot. On the bright side, at least the coun-

cil's anger is no longer directed toward us. I don't know about you, but I'm feeling a lot better about our odds of returning home safely tonight.

"I'd be surprised if Liam hasn't put one of those all points bulletins out on us," my mother muttered, her gaze going beyond the four council members in front of us. We *had* been gone a long time. Liam wouldn't have stayed in the truck, which meant he was out patrolling a neighborhood of witches and warlocks who might not appreciate his presence. Nausea hit me hard. "How did you figure out it was Hestia?"

Yeah, I'd like to know that one, too.

"The bug that was crawling around on the ground wasn't an average insect," I shared, remembering when Leo had sent the six-legged creature sailing through the air with just one swipe. "It was Harold, the cockroach. He is Hestia's familiar, and he was listening in on our conversation with Angelica. I put two and two together, and also recalled how she was so focused on the vision she had of her death."

Harold. That creepy, crawly little bugger. Where did he go?

"Angelica did seem aggravated that we continued to accuse the council," my mother summarized, once again scanning the distance behind the four arguing council members. What or who was she looking for? "Hestia's crimes should be dealt with by her own coven. Our task is to collect Strifle and be on our way as soon as possible."

Too little, too late. Hold onto your hats, folks! I'm pretty sure we're about to meet the fifth council member.

Eighteen

Leo hadn't been kidding when he told us we should hold onto our hats—not that we had any hats on our heads, which I initially regretted. I'd left my watch cap in the truck. My adrenaline had spiked and instantly caused another hot flash upon seeing a beautiful older woman walking toward us from the front entrance.

Could this day get any worse? Forget I said that. We're still at some risk of becoming little green amphibian lumps of Jell-O with legs.

"I apologize for my delay, but I was busy keeping a certain human occupied from scouring the neighborhood for our guests." The woman was easily in her seventies, but age hadn't altered one ounce of her physical beauty. She definitely had to be dabbling with the age spells to look that good. I would have wanted to know more about her had stark terror not spiked through my heart at the mention of a *certain human*. He could be none other than Liam. "Would someone like to catch me up with our friends here?"

In a net, maybe. You and your group of bumbling band of cohorts have got a lot of explaining to do.

"Is that you, Benny?" the woman asked nonchalantly before wiping away a snowflake that had fallen on the shoulder of her long black dress coat. "Ever the gentleman, I see. You haven't changed much in a lifetime. It's been at least that long, don't you think?"

Rowena, it hasn't been nearly long enough for me. And it's Mr. Leo to you now.

"Mom?"

I'd never met my great-aunt before, but something about her commanded attention—everyone's attention. She carried herself as if she was mystical royalty, even having that tilt of her chin that could only come from a sense of being highborn.

Perfect angle for someone to—

"I don't believe it," Regina muttered in shock, yanking on my arm until I was forced to take a step back. "Aunt Rowena."

Could we please get on with this? I need to clean my fur.

"Rowena, you aren't needed here," Merrick announced with irritation, torn between keeping his gaze on Hestia versus my aunt's distracting entrance. Ruby was still wringing her hands, and Angelica appeared like she wanted to bare those nails and use them as claws. There was definitely no love lost between the so-called fifth member and the rest of the council. "Your replacement on the council is forthcoming, as well as your banishment."

I might be able to stay for another few moments if there's going to be entertainment.

Leo was getting enjoyment out of Rowena's displacement within the coven, but I wasn't so sure it hadn't been orchestrated on purpose. After all, Angelica had admitted to Aunt

Rowena heading the faction who was currently opposing the remaining members of council.

"It's her!" Hestia exclaimed, fanning herself with her right hand even though I could literally see my breath as I breathed out. "Oh, Rowena...how could you? You've set me up. Stealing those artifacts was your idea. You wanted me to take the fall all along! Merrick, do something."

There was movement in my peripheral vision, and it was none other than Harold scurrying past us as fast as a cockroach could scamper. He was heading past us, toward the large knobby tree where Angelica had first gone behind to check on the coven's cherished relics. I would have followed had I not been worried about the anarchy running amuck with the council. I half-expected spells to start flying any moment.

I've got Harold in my sights. Do you want me to dispatch him with my pointy claws or my sharp teeth?

Sure enough, Leo was hunched down on all fours. There was no short-term or long-term memory loss hampering him now. He was in all his hunting glory, wiggling his butt like those adorable kittens on social media.

Don't get me wrong. With all his tufts of hair pointing every which a way, his tail that resembled more of the shape of a clothes hanger, and his left eye bulging in excitement...let's just say he resembled a cat high on catnip stuck to the grill of a Mack truck.

Three, two, one...

Leo darted after Harold, disappearing behind the thick trunk while using the old benches as catapults.

"Until such time my coveted spot on the council is filled, the coven's problems are still officially my business," Rowena declared, completely ignoring Hestia's accusations and drawing my attention back to the confrontation at hand. She flicked those oh-so-familiar green eyes toward the accused. With one step, she had Hestia backing away from the group. "Shall we?"

I had no idea what Rowena was proposing, but the way my mother's grasp tightened on my hand told me we didn't want to be near the group. As a matter of fact, we didn't stop walking backward until the backs of our knees touched those benches I'd been telling you about.

"Take notice," Mom warned me, never once taking her focus off her aunt. "A witch can place a protection spell on herself so that another witch or warlock has difficulty breaking through their shield. But when four experienced and rather powerful beings work together, let's just say those barriers aren't enough to protect oneself completely."

"They're going to use a truth incantation, aren't they?" I muttered, looking across to see there had to be at least twenty feet between us and them. Mom had made sure that we weren't in the area of effect of the magic they'd be using to break through Hestia's protection spell. This meant I had time to follow Leo and Harold. Hopefully, that little critter was heading directly toward Strifle. "I'll be back."

My mother wasn't expecting me to sneak away so suddenly. The chant continued to flow from the four council members, leaving Hestia pleading for their mercy. Hopefully, their objective took a few moments and allowed me to finally locate Strifle.

Harold wasn't heavy enough to cause impressions in the thin layer of snow, but one couldn't miss Leo's pawprints. His weight had him sinking deep into to the light layer of snow, let alone evidence of his awkward pouncing after his prey here and there.

...busted! It's over, Harold. Scurry your creepy legs away from the cage.

I wasn't expecting the sight before me. I'd followed Leo's paw prints around the large oak tree only to find an antique table full of beautiful relics, from gold and silver vessels to hand-carved wooden bowls. It was like walking into a treasure trove of magical artifacts. I wasn't sure where to look first. That was...until Leo spoke again.

Get away from the tree, Harold. Scram!

Benny, you haven't changed. You've always thought of yourself as high and mighty, but look at you now. I'll take my six legs and shiny wings over your muddled disarray of fur any day!

Why you little—

Leo and Harold continued to argue with one another, but Harold's little antennas stood on end. It was hard to see his face, considering he was so small, but I was pretty sure his mouth was twitching.

Hestia!

Harold scurried away so fast that I jumped to the side to avoid having his creepy legs running across my boots. I hadn't been sure why Leo was all but demanding Harold step away from a smaller tree behind the table until he tentatively reached out with his paw. Sure enough, Leo's right front leg went through the bark of the tree as if it were a mirage.

I knew it! Harold was protecting this tree as if his life depended on it. Trust me, it took all of my considerable restraint not to squash that beady-eyed bug with one swipe. I think I'll send a can of Raid for his next birthday.

"Don't be so mean," I chided, kneeling next to him as we still stared at the tree. I couldn't help but test what I'd seen Leo do with his paw, only to find that the tree was indeed real. What wasn't tangible was a small hollowed out section near the ground. "Hestia, and Harold by extension, will be going through a trial of their peers in this coven. Harold's job is to protect Hestia, so have a little sympathy. Remember, whatever happens to her happens to him."

You always have to ruin my fun, don't you? You won't find me consorting with the likes of him anytime soon.

Leo shuddered before sitting back on his haunches.

Cockroaches are just creepy. With that said, I'd hate to be in his shoes when they finish with Hestia.

"Leo, what are we going to find?" I couldn't help but be hesitant to reach my hand through the false mirage that was the base of the small tree. Seeing a ghost was one thing, but I wasn't sure I could deal with watching a beautiful little fairy pass away. My chest tightened in pain for what the familiar had to be going through, but even worse...her upcoming death should I free her from her restraints. "I'm not sure I can do this."

It's not what you think. Go ahead, Raven. It will be okay.

It's happened a time or two before, but it was rare that Leo's tone softened to the point I felt as if he were truly encouraging me in this witchcraft journey. It was hard not to get sentimental kneeling by his side.

Don't go getting soppy on me. Put your hand in there, for supernatural sake.

Still worried about Liam and wondering what Aunt Rowena had done or said to him, I didn't waste any more time. I held my breath as I reached through the illusion of bark, my fingers coming into contact with something cold and sharp.

Well? Is it Strifle?

"It feels like metal."

Pull it out.

"What if we find—"

Leo didn't waste time and stuck his head through the

magical veil. Within seconds, he was back on his haunches and twitching his whiskers.

It's a vessel, Raven. Now drag it out here so we can do what we've come to do and leave this place before we're sitting next to Hestia and Harold in some magical jail cell hoping to make bail.

How would I explain that to Liam? That question alone had me wrapping my fingers around the cold metal container and dragging it through the illusion of bark.

Your nose is red.

"What?"

Your nose is red. I'm just pointing that out. Hey, what's in the box?

Leo's short-term memory had kicked in with a bang, but I'm sure it wouldn't last long...especially when he got a good look at his surroundings.

Ohhhhh, pretty!

Leo was describing the warm glow coming from the translucent square of gleaming gold. My gaze was glued to the golden hue, and my eyes began to adjust to the brightness emanating from within. Through the thin delicate walls of the magical vessel, I could see a beautiful blonde creature lying on her side with striking wings that were an array of pastel shades that actually glimmered.

She was an incredibly amazing sight.

Hey, Strifle! What are you doing all cooped up in there? The tiny pixie had no strength to pick herself up upon hearing Leo's voice. Her struggle pulled at my heart strings, and I unconsciously reached out and opened the lid to the mystical container.

I wasn't expecting anything magical to happen. I just wanted to be able to take Strifle out of her prison and comfort her, but what took place next was breathtaking.

Strifle's magnificent wings began to lift, and her body gradually floated behind the iridescent extensions. It was impossible not to fall back into the thin layer of snow next to Leo as the charming fairy burst forth from her confinement.

There was no sadness.

There was no time to grieve.

Strifle stretched her tiny arms above her head as if she'd been asleep for days, eventually giving the cutest laugh I'd ever heard. A glowing trail of glimmers followed her in circles as she spun around and around, her giggles floating through the air as she suddenly combusted into a shower of fairy dust.

Hmpfh. Well, that was anticlimactic.

Leo flicked his paw to shake off the colorful shower of glitter left behind by Strifle. Nothing happened. He shook his paw again and again until he realized that Strifle had left behind what looked to be the smallest pink kiss on his fur. It was her thank you to him. His tail flicked in irritation, telling me his memory had returned.

Pixies—they're nothing but trouble. I keep telling you, but you won't listen. Now look at what she's gone and done. It's going to take a lot of cleaning before this nasty stuff wears off.

Nineteen

"What did we miss?" I asked breathlessly, having quickly made my way back to where my mother still stood watching Hestia beg for forgiveness. At least she hadn't been turned into a toad. "By the way, Strifle is with Mazie now. At least, I think that's where she disappeared to. Let's just say she left behind a lot of fairy dust."

This stuff better come off. Maybe some acetone will work. Do we have any nail polish remover back at the house?

"The council eventually used a truth spell on Hestia," Mom replied softly, gesturing toward the blubbering woman. "It's a shame, really. The woman saw her own death and did everything in the world to prevent an act she had no idea of when it would happen, regardless of whether it was tomorrow or twenty years down the road."

Twenty years might be a stretch at this point.

"Isn't it human nature to fight against the icy grip of death?" I sure wasn't ready to cross through the veil. Sure, Mazie seemed happy enough to be where she was, but it wasn't like she'd had a choice in the matter. Now that I think about it,

Strifle had gone in a puff of giggles. There was a chance it wasn't so bad on the other side, but I'd still like to put off the inevitable for as long as possible. "What will happen to Hestia now?"

Banished...maybe as a toad.

Ruby was ever the loyal friend with her arm wrapped around Hestia, trying to reassure her that everything was going to be okay. I wasn't so sure that was the truth.

"Mr. Leo, you can rest assured that we have never handed down a sentence of that magnitude. Those are just old witch's tales," Merrick reassured us, presumably having been listening to every word that passed between Leo, my mother, and me. Angelica was nodding in decisive agreement, though I wouldn't put it past her to bring back some of those old witch's tales. "Hestia will stand trial for those crimes she committed against the coven, along with the abduction and torture of a precious familiar. I suppose we should thank you for your...interference."

If he wasn't such a powerful warlock, I might have something to say about his inability to express gratitude properly.

"Merrick, I don't understand." Mom had taken a step forward in confusion, but I made sure to keep ahold of the back of her coat. Regardless of the offhand thanks we'd been given for discovering who was behind the thefts from the temple and the abduction of Strifle, I wasn't so sure the older warlock had our best intentions in mind. After all, the Marigolds weren't welcome in this coven after my grandmother had consorted with a human...and now Aunt Rowena. Technically, the same went for my exploits. "Why are you splintering the coven in two? You used to be so understanding back when I sought you out for answers."

"We're losing our power, Regina," Merrick responded with

a despondent frown. "We grow weaker and weaker with each generation. We aren't the only coven or council that feels our magic slipping away in this manner. Something must be done. We must return to our roots or we will perish."

In case you missed it, the old warlock is hinting that you should kick the good ol' sheriff to the curb.

No wonder Nan had left the coven. Liam and I hadn't even had our second date, and I couldn't fathom walking away from him.

You're assuming Rowena left him in one piece.

"Maybe if you hadn't excommunicated so many members for insignificant infractions, the coven wouldn't be in this predicament." My mother stepped forward and grasped the warlock's weathered hands. "Merrick, it doesn't have to be all or nothing."

"But it does, dear. You're blind to what is coming. I am not."

"Nonsense," Rowena interrupted rather haughtily, having been off to the side listening to the exchange. "There are other ways to regain our powers, but you're resistant to anyone's counsel but that witch you call a wife."

That was pretty far below the belt.

I'm almost positive that Angelica would have commenced some type of witchcraft battle against Rowena had Merrick not rested his hand on her arm to stave off such retaliation. Rowena arched a brow in mockery, almost daring Angelica to follow through with her original intentions.

Did you see that taunting look? I'm beginning to remember why your grandmother loathed her sister. Yes, it's all coming back to me now.

"I'd like a word in privacy with my niece and great-niece, if you don't mind." Rowena didn't leave Merrick or Angelica much room to argue with her. "Seeing as my seat on the council is about to be filled sooner rather than later, I'll leave you to deal with Hestia. Now, if you'll excuse us?"

Mom reluctantly stepped back. It was evident she wanted to talk more with Merrick, but he'd already turned away to speak with the other council members about what to do with Hestia until the trial could be held.

"You're definitely a Marigold, aren't you?" Rowena muttered as she raked her gaze up and down my form. "Hair, eyes, cheekbones...hips. Yes, you're a Marigold, all right."

Hit her with an energy ball, Raven. We need to gain the initiative here.

"I've heard a lot about you, Aunt Rowena. I'm sad that so much family drama has gotten in the way of family."

Ahhh, the guilt trip approach. A classic, yet still effective. I like your style, Raven.

A flash of emotion flickered in Aunt Rowena's green eyes for just a second, though my objective hadn't been to guilt her into anything. I truly meant what I said, and I was still open to having some type of relationship with her.

Are you out of your blasted mind?

"I need the two of you to listen very closely," Aunt Rowena cautioned, completely ignoring my attempt to reconnect my family. She made sure that her back was to the other council members, even going so far as to look around us...maybe for familiars? I wasn't sure, but I did as she instructed. "This coven *is* going to war, and there is no avoiding your involvement."

She doesn't know us very well, does she? Oh, wait. That's right. I had to get stuck with Scooby Doo. I don't even like dogs.

"You'll be forced to choose a side." Aunt Rowena continued to speak as if Leo hadn't uttered a word, her voice becoming rather ominous. "I have no doubt you'll fall in line with the faction I've gathered to take control of this council that has seen fit to replace me. Well, there will be no council of elders by the time I'm done."

I believe we should take that as our cue to exit stage left. We want no part of this coup d'état.

"Times *have* changed." Rowena purposefully glanced over her shoulder to point out her current obstacles. "We must do the same or our kind will cease to exist. Do not believe Merrick or the others when they say differently. Now, I must go before the tenuous string of peace snaps and someone does something they'll regret. The open battle has yet to begin in earnest."

Your string of peace is an illusion. There hasn't been peace in this coven since before I lost my first life here defending my sovereignty.

My mother and I hadn't been given time to ask Aunt Rowena any questions. I would have loved to have inquired about the one phone call she'd placed to Nan years ago. You know the one I'm talking about. It was regarding bread or some such thing.

Don't give Rowena a chance to talk you into joining her army that she's apparently put together. I already told you that I don't look good in camouflage.

"Oh, and Regina?" Aunt Rowena called over her shoulder as she continued to walk away. "I left a gift for you with that handsome specimen near the front gate. Maybe next time you won't wait so long to come calling on your aunt. And Raven? You've made me proud."

A toad. If she's left a toad in the truck, you're taking it with you back to the city, Regina. I want no such creature in my house. I have enough on my plate dealing with Ted—the clay playboy.

"What are we going to say to Liam?" I asked worriedly, walking briskly through the numerous snow-covered yards as my mother and I made our way back to the front of the neighborhood. "He's going to know we're lying to him. This is horrible."

The good ol' sheriff doesn't look very happy, either.

Leo's observation came due to his not wanting to trudge through any more snow. He was already at the truck, and his opinion about Liam almost had me stopping me in my tracks. The shove my mother gave me wouldn't allow it.

What do you know? There's no toad.

"Aunt Rowena assured us that she'd taken care of Liam." There wasn't a lot of confidence in my mother's statement, which had me quickening my step. I had no idea how long we'd been gone, so it was hard to judge what little itsy white lie I would have to come up with to explain our absence. "I'm not sure I trust her, but she does seem to be on the right side of this war that is brewing within the coven."

Oh, there's going to be a war, all right. Wait until your mother sees what Rowena left behind.

"There shouldn't even be a conflict." It was ridiculous to even speak the words, let alone have Leo egging on more family feuds. Seriously. A war between the family of witches and warlocks? "The coven is a community, and they should all work together. If our powers are weakening, then we should band together...not fight one another. And Aunt Rowena seemed to want us in her life. Would it be so bad to reconnect with her?"

In a single word? Yes.

"I hate to admit it, but I agree with Leo." My mother side-stepped a garden gnome that had seen better days. "Your grandmother always said that Aunt Rowena had an agenda of some sort. We don't want any part of a war, and we certainly don't want to be beholden to her for any reason."

We were almost to the street where Liam's truck was parked, but I had to slow our pace when the shadows of the houses made it hard to see the ground in front of us. It was a good thing, too. Otherwise, I might have gotten severe frostbite with Mazie's sudden appearance.

You tell that tea-drinking witch we've solved her case. She can repay us by telling the other unsettled spirits that we're out of the investigative business. Our doors are closed.

"Mazie, you can't be here," I whispered, hoping that Liam stayed in the truck. Peering through Mazie's floral dress and matching teacup, I could see the front grill of his F150. "Liam is going to—"

"I don't know how I can ever repay you, Raven," Mazie gushed, fairy dust glowing in the dark despite my warning that Liam might catch sight of something that would scar him for life. "You've given me back my precious Strifle."

Hey, ask that pixie tyrant how I get this fairy dust off my fur!

Strifle's high-pitched laughter filled the air, along with another shower of pink and turquoise hues showering the darkened night. She was very pleased with herself for marking Leo. Mazie just smiled and held up her teacup in salute before more than repaying any amount of money I could have put into an invoice.

"Rosemary wishes more than anything that she were here with the three of you."

Oh, I miss that woman.

My mother's hand covered her heart and a tiny squeak escaped her lips that revealed how touched she was by Nan's sentiment.

I'm not crying. Are you?

"She also wanted me to tell you that Rowena will need all of your help in the coming year, and she's asking that all of you let bygones be bygones." Mazie and Strifle both began to fade, but not before she finished speaking. "That includes Mr. Leo! Please tell him that Strifle left something behind to help when the time comes..."

What's that supposed to mean? Hey, tell those two tricksters to get back here! They can't drop a bomb like that and think it's okay to just vanish.

Mazie and Strifle seemed to believe otherwise, and they both eventually faded into the dark night.

Leave it to a pixie and her witch to ruin a perfectly good ending.

"Well," my mother declared, clearing her throat as she composed herself. She had been harboring guilt over not making up for lost time and being at odds with Nan for years. I was happy she'd been given a message from beyond. I wasn't sure if fate existed, but I do believe Mazie came to me and Leo for a reason...and maybe it was to heal old wounds within the Marigold family. "Shall we continue on before Liam decides to leave without us? Let's hope that Aunt Rowena took care of all the loose ends."

Trust me, Rowena did that and more.

Leo was beginning to worry me by not telling us what Aunt Rowena had done, especially if she hadn't come up with some plausible explanation for Liam to believe. Was this it? Would we even be given a chance to have dinner Friday night?

You can always stay at home with me. I've got no plans. I'll let you share my pipe.

We finally cleared the last yard and practically spilled into the street right next to the front gate. I immediately breathed a sigh of relief to find Liam standing next to his truck with his cell phone next to his ear. He appeared worried, but relief filled his handsome features at the sight of me.

Fine. Go to dinner with him. Just so you know, I'm not sharing my pipe with Ted.

Tonight had been quite emotional, and I couldn't stop moving my feet and walking right into his embrace. I inhaled his scent as I wrapped my arms around his neck, ignoring that I would have to explain my overreaction at some point.

"Your great aunt said that you went to visit one of your grandmother's old friends who isn't doing well," Liam murmured against my hair, wrapping his arms around my waist as he pulled me closer. I couldn't resist closing my eyes and soaking in his warmth. The cold must have gotten to me without me realizing how much. "I'm sorry, Raven. I'm sure it brought up memories that you'd rather forget."

Liam had to be referring to my practically nonexistent relationship with Nan. In a way, he was right. Seeing Aunt Rowena and knowing that old family feuds had kept all of us apart had been difficult to face. The security of his embrace had been needed more than I'd realized.

"Thanks for waiting," I whispered, grateful that my mother and Leo hadn't said a word while I had taken a bit of refuge in Liam's arms. "I'm sorry we took so long."

Liam studied me carefully after I'd slowly pulled away, and I smiled to reassure him that I was okay. And I was, especially knowing that Aunt Rowena had kept her word.

I can't remain silent anymore. That brief stint almost killed me. Rowena? Keep her word? Oh, are you in for a treat! I only stayed long enough to see the look on your mother's face, but I'm going to have to meet you at home. I'm not riding in that truck with that...thing.

"It was no problem." Liam looked over my shoulder to

where my mom stood with her arms wrapped around her waist. "Ms. Marigold, let's get you inside the truck with Strifle. I'm sure she'll calm down once she sees you. I'm glad you and your aunt worked things out, and it was very nice of her to invite me inside for a cup of coffee."

"Strifle?" Mom had tried her best not to act surprised. She didn't succeed, but she did cover it up by placing her well-manicured hand over her mouth as if she were overcome with emotion. "Oh, that's just wonderful news. Isn't it, Raven?"

I could only nod and follow behind Liam as he closed the distance to the driver's side door. He opened it before doing the same to the slim back door where the dome light shone brightly on...

You guessed it.

Leo was very pleased with himself, so I'm hoping you did guess what was going to be in the backseat.

They're smart, Raven. Give them the credit that is due.

"Oh look, dear," my mother exclaimed, the stress in the tone of her voice evident. "It's Strifle...my sugar glider."

That cackling sound I heard was definitely Leo laughing, in spite of him sounding like he was choking to death on a hairball.

There, in a beautifully crafted carrier cage, was the cutest little sugar glider I'd ever seen. Well, I've never really seen a sugar glider in person. It didn't matter. He was still the most adorable looking creature with the biggest greenish yellow eyes that blinked slowly as he watched us carefully from his carrier.

Does this mean war? If so, I'm going to need time to pop some popcorn and settle in with my pipe. These future battles are going to be epic entertainment!

~ The End ~

Compelling love spells are used to brew up one charmingly delightful whodunit as USA Today Bestselling Author Kennedy Layne continues her cozy paranormal mystery series...

Boxes of delicious chocolates and roses by the dozen are aplenty in the small town of Paramour Bay as Valentine's Day approaches, but all is not so rosy in Raven Marigold's life when a simple love enchantment goes horribly awry. You see, the affection spell is only meant to affect one recipient...not the entire town!

Things for Raven go from bad to worse when small fires begin to break out all around town, causing damages to the local shops and homes alike. What's a witch to do when she believes her attempt at evocation magic might be responsible for sparking these crimes? Why, she must grab her trusty familiar and investigate, of course!

Open your hearts to this spellbinding Valentine's Day tale by falling in love with this charming adventure of mischief, tea, and magic!

Other Series By Kennedy Layne

Detective Kinsley Aspen Novels

Touch of Evil Series

The Graveside Mysteries

The Widow Taker Trilogy

Paramour Bay Mysteries

Hex on Me Mysteries

The Safeguard Series

Keys to Love Series

Office Roulette Trilogy

Surviving Ashes Series

Red Starr Series

CSA Case Files

About the Author

Kennedy Layne, a USA Today bestselling author, resides in the Midwest with her retired Marine Master Sergeant husband and their menagerie of pets. Fueled by coffee and her love for thrillers, cozy mysteries, and romantic suspense novels, Kennedy loves to spend time in front of her fireplace crafting stories that keep her readers guessing until the very end.

Email:
kennedylayneauthor@gmail.com

Website:
www.kennedylayne.com

Newsletter:
www.kennedylayne.com/newsletter.html

www.ingramcontent.com/pod-product-compliance
Lightning Source LLC
Chambersburg PA
CBHW070308280626
47159CB00018B/3179